USA TODAY BESTSELLING AUTHOR

Dale Mayer

TERK'S GUARDIANS

RIFF 15

RIFF: TERK'S GUARDIANS, BOOK 15
Beverly Dale Mayer
Valley Publishing Ltd.

ISBN-13: 978-1-778867-06-4
Print Edition

Books in This Series:

About This Book

At Terk's request, Jonas had discreetly delved into the mystery surrounding the murder of Riff's fiancée and unearthed a crucial piece of information that could shatter the case wide open. For Riff, the frustration involved in finding the murderer is palpable. He would have taken action much sooner, if only this information had come to light earlier. Yet it had been buried in silence, unnoticed, … until now.

Angela had harbored a complex mix of love and resentment for Riff for years. He had been her sister's fiancé, leaving Angela with no choice but to keep her feelings hidden. After her sister's tragic murder, Riff spiraled into darkness, consumed by his quest for answers. Angela sought the truth as well, but she knew that her presence was a painful reminder of his loss—a tension neither of them could ignore.

As the long-buried answers begin to surface, the new information is nothing like what either of them expected, propelling them into a perilous journey toward the truth. Amid the danger, an unexpected bond forms between them, adding a layer of complexity to their shared mission. Together they must navigate a treacherous path, where every revelation brings them closer to both the truth and each other.

Sign up to be notified of all Dale's releases here!

https://geni.us/DaleNews

PROLOGUE

TERK PICKED UP his favorite mug and filled it with coffee, then grabbed a second mug and filled it as well. With both cups in hand, he headed over to a couple easy chairs that sat in front of the fireplace. He handed one coffee cup to Jonas.

Jonas accepted it gratefully. "It's a hell of a spot to be in," he muttered, taking a sip, then sinking into the chair, cuddling in against the fireplace. "Life is pretty tough here for you guys, isn't it?"

"Let's just say, we've come through the worst of it, and we're pretty happy where we've landed," Terk clarified in a somewhat neutral tone.

Jonas gave him a sideways look. "I do understand, you know?"

"Good," Terk replied, "because most of us have been to hell and back, so trust doesn't come that easy."

"Right, I understand that too," he murmured, "and, in many cases, with good reason."

"What about you? Did you find more moles?"

"We did," he admitted in an abashed tone. "Unfortunately another guy in MI5 was working with the new hire in MI6," he added, with a wave of his hand. "We figure more snitches are on the payroll at the hotels we are known to use, so we're following up on all that too. Regardless, with both of our in-house moles tossed out, we're hoping for an easier time going forward."

"Until the next one."

Jonas nodded, as he stared down at his cup. "The sad thing is, there's always a next one, isn't there?"

Terk looked over at him and nodded. "There is. We keep thinking that we're finally at a stage where everything will be fine. Then something happens, and it's not fine anymore."

"And here I was hoping you had good news."

"Oh, I have lots of good news, just not necessarily anything that matters to you," Terk noted. "I get that you're here for healing, and believe me that the gals will do the best they can for you. However, I feel as if something else is behind your visit—something deeper."

Jonas looked around to see if anyone was nearby. "You asked me to look into a certain matter a while back."

Terk shifted and straightened. "I did."

"I've got some interesting information."

"What's that?"

"The private investigator hired to look into the case was murdered not long after starting the investigation."

Terk frowned at him. "That's not in my files."

"No, that's because the family didn't want it made public."

"Yet that's a big point in terms of what happened to Riff's fiancée. That PI was the one actively trying to find out what happened to her. So, if he was murdered and not killed in a car accident, as Riff was told, that's a big deal."

"He was run over in a deliberate act, but there are no answers, no leads. We have nothing to point to who did it."

"That makes me wonder if it was a professional hit."

"Oh, don't worry. It makes me wonder the same thing," Jonas confirmed. "I get that it's very important, and, for some people involved, like Riff, it's beyond important. But that PI case was closed, and nobody's willing to open it because it's already been assessed and declared an accident. However, a new look says it's a deliberate hit-and-run. We also have a family member saying they received a threatening letter that, if they pursued this any further, somebody else in the family would die."

"*Great*," Terk muttered. "So, chances are, the private eye was on to something."

"Exactly. So, what I do have and I admit it's not a whole lot," Jonas conceded, as he reached into his pocket and pulled out a USB key. "is what we found on the investigator's computer at the time of his death."

Terk reached out a hand, taking the key, and nodded. "Thank you, Jonas."

"I don't know that it will be of any help."

"No, but, if it gives us even one more little bit of information, it's important. No matter how small, it's still a piece of the puzzle, and we need it."

At that moment, Riff walked in, his gaze going to the two of them. He joined them, frowning, looking down at Jonas's leg. "How bad is it?"

"It will be fine, given a little time," Jonas replied, with a formal tone. "Thanks for the assistance in the tunnel."

Riff nodded. "No problem. That's the way the world is supposed to work, right?"

At that, Terk held out his hand with the USB key. "Riff, Jonas came for a little healing assistance, but he also brought this for you."

Riff stared at it, as if it would bite him. He looked from

one man to the other and back again cautiously, as if he knew already. "What is it?"

Jonas replied, "It's the contents of the private eye's personal effects and computer files and diary at the time of his murder."

It took Riff a moment to blink his way through that. "*Murder.* It was declared an accident."

"That's how the family wanted it portrayed and reported. I spoke with them recently, and they received a death threat in a letter just prior to a public announcement about the loss of their family member. The letter promised the immediate death of another family member if they didn't go along with the accidental death report on the PI and didn't drop all attempts to prove it was anything other than an unfortunate car accident."

He stared at Jonas in shock. "So, you're saying the investigator was murdered."

"That's our belief, yes," Jonas confirmed. "I figured you would want first crack at it."

He snatched the USB key from Terk's hand and stared down at it, his jaw working. Just then Angela walked into the room. He looked over at her. "You always seem to turn up just at the most inconvenient time."

"Or the right time," she argued, staring at the USB key. "Did I just hear what I thought I heard?"

He nodded. "Apparently. ... I don't know what's on here yet." He looked back at Jonas.

Jonas shrugged. "I don't either," he admitted. "But one good turn deserves another, so thank you for keeping me alive back there in the tunnels. I have a hunch you may have done more than just pack me out." When he saw the quick grin cross Riff's face, Jonas nodded. "Let's hope this helps your hunt."

As Riff headed out of the room, he looked back at Terk and announced, "I'll go check this out."

Terk nodded.

Angela rushed to follow Riff, calling out, "Wait for me."

He looked back at her and frowned. "You know you don't need to be involved in this."

She glared at him. "I lost someone too. She was my sister, after all."

He hesitated, then nodded. "Fine, but it's unlikely you'll be happy with anything we find."

"I haven't been happy about anything over the last five years to date," she added bitterly. "So at least let me find some closure."

He hesitated, then turned to Terk, who nodded. Riff sighed. "Fine, but don't blame me if you don't like where this ends up."

"I won't blame you at all," she declared.

He laughed. "That would be a first. So far, you've done nothing but." And, with that, he turned and walked out.

She now cast a glance back at Terk.

Terk again nodded. "If you don't go, you won't ever get answers. If I *must* weigh in, don't let him push you around."

She snorted. "I haven't ever let him push me around so far," she declared. "Damn, I've all but moved into your place, trying to stay close, and all he does is try to push me away."

"He needs answers first," Terk noted, his tone steady as he studied her. "Give him some room but maybe not too much."

She nodded and flashed him a bright grin. "Thanks." And, with that, she was gone.

Jonas groaned at his side. "Young love. ... Nothing hurts

quite like that."

Terk looked over at him and nodded. "Particularly with star-crossed lovers like these two, but maybe now they can finally find some answers about the past and can head into the future."

"I hope so. … Now, what about you running a government department for me?"

Terk sighed. Jonas was apparently still serious about this, given everything they had been through. "If I take it up with the team and if they all say yes, I *might* be interested," Terk explained. "But you know for a fact that every fricking one of them will say not only no but *hell no*." Then he gave Jonas a fat smile. "Let's just continue the way we are for now. Maybe before long we'll have Riff's case fully closed, and I can get him to come on board full-time."

"He's good, isn't he?" Jonas asked, as he studied the doorway the two had gone through.

"He's one of the best," Terk replied. "He just doesn't believe it. Something, … well, finding these answers," he added, "will make all the difference."

"I hope so." Jonas looked far off into the distance. "The world is a mess out there, and, if we don't have people like you and me and them to straighten out all the problems, … it'll only get worse."

And, with that, the two men raised their coffee mugs, clanked them together, and each had a sip. Terk noted, "You know, if you didn't have a busted-up leg, we could be drinking whiskey."

Jonas stared down at his coffee mug and then frowned at him and declared, "I don't have a busted-up leg."

Terk laughed, then got up and grabbed the whiskey bottle from the nearby shelf, quickly pouring a healthy slug into each cup. "Now, let's have some proper coffee."

And together they sat here and enjoyed the moment.

CHAPTER 1

RIFF STARED AT the file he had quickly printed from the USB drive Jonas had brought for him. Riff was in his room with the door closed, but he knew Angela would be here any minute. He was hoping to get through the file in privacy, specifically without her looking over his shoulder. He knew that wasn't fair, considering they had both suffered over Sadie's death. Angela had lost her sister, but he had lost his fiancée, his future, and he'd been holding the grudge for God-only-knows how long.

When a hard pounding on the door began, he groaned. "Come in."

It slammed open as Angela stormed in, glaring at him. "Would you really try to hide this from me?" she asked, pointing to the pages in front of him.

"No, of course not," he muttered, trying hard to be patient with her. "I was just hoping to read through it first, so I could summarize it for you."

She rolled her eyes at that. "I can read pretty well myself, you know?" she snapped, as she walked over and sat down beside him, eyeing the file. "It's not a lot, is it?"

"No, it's not," he agreed, "but something here is of value."

"What's that?"

"One of the witnesses I had tried to talk to at the

time, … he ended up in jail in London. He was pretty pissed at that and didn't want anything to do with me. He personally had nothing at all to do with the case, but one of his cellmates offered some new information."

"Let's go then," she declared, jumping to her feet. "No point in waiting here if the information is in London."

"The guy's been transferred a couple times recently, and that news didn't get relayed to us. We'll track down where he's at right now, and that will take some patience. Before you rave on, we're doing everything we need to do and have also pulled Jonas in on it."

"Interesting," she noted, staring at him. "Sadie wasn't the kind of person to want all this nightmare."

"No, she wasn't," he replied, studying her. "We haven't talked about her very much in the last few years."

"Not anything to talk about. We were waiting for closure," she stated, staring at him. "Hell, I still am."

"So am I," he said impatiently, gathering the printed copy as he stood up. "We're both looking for closure. When this shit happens, there is no life until we get answers."

"Unless you make a life," she suggested, shooting him a look. "You can't just hide behind guilt and any other excuse you can dream up."

He stiffened and glared at her, but she glared right back. That was the thing about Angela. She had absolutely no reservations about sticking up that chin of hers and getting herself into trouble for all the right reasons. He could almost admire it, but he really didn't need her on his case right now.

She shrugged. "You know I'm right, and you've used her death as an excuse to stop living a full life. Now that you may find some answers," she added, nodding her head, "I hope you can get back to the land of the living. Oh, and I'm coming with you to interview the witness. Don't think for a moment I'm not."

"It would be a lot easier if I went alone," he explained but knew it would be futile. She was always a force to be contended with, but, when on a mission, she was unstoppable.

"Yeah, … that's not happening."

"What about your patients?" he asked, with a mocking grin. "Are there babies somewhere around the world who need you?"

"Plenty of babies around the world need me," she declared, "but sometimes you have to do what you need to do for yourself." And, with a pointed look at him, she walked back out to the hallway, turning at the last moment. "Don't even think about leaving without me. I'll go pack a bag."

"I haven't confirmed where our jailbird is yet. Regardless London is hardly anything we have to pack a bag for," he noted in exasperation, as he carefully closed the door to his suite behind him.

"Maybe not, but any time you guys head out for what seems to be a simple job, it ends up taking a lot longer. I don't want to be without at least one change of clothes." She rolled her eyes as she spoke, and he could hardly deny her statement. "Do not make the mistake of thinking you can take off without me." And, with that, she turned in the opposite direction and headed toward her bedroom, at least the designated room she used when she came to help with the babies and to do all the maternity and new-baby check-ups.

He still didn't quite understand how she managed to get into this whole deal at Terk's place, with the pregnancies and beyond, but considering the number of babies born in the castle, it did make some sense. And, … he hated to admit it, she wouldn't let him get very far away. She was just as invested in justice for her sister's death as he was, even more so. Immediately shaking his head, he muttered to himself, "Hell no, not *more so*. Not in a million years."

But Angela's dig at his old guilt had definitely found a home, and it wasn't the first time she had accused him of such a thing. It was all he could do sometimes to stop the guilt from choking him. Maybe Angela was right. Maybe it was just for the sake of relieving his guilt that he needed closure. He needed a way out, so he could walk toward something else in life and find another reason to move forward.

So far, all his searches and hunting down leads hadn't turned up much, each hopeful find became just another dead end. Although, as he stared down at the file with new info gathered by Jonas, a grin appeared on Riff's face. For the first time in a very long while, he realized that he might get some answers after all.

He headed down to the kitchen and into the massive dining room by the fireplace, where Terkel and several of the other team members sat around the table.

Immediately Royce jumped up. When Riff frowned at him, Royce shrugged. "Hey, you've helped us, and we're here to help you."

Riff shook his head. "Not happening."

At that, Royce, his voice calm and patient, shrugged again, and added, "That's too bad because you're not going into this alone."

"No, he's not," confirmed the woman behind him. In came Angela, with an overnight bag slung over her shoulder.

Riff eyed her and her bag and asked, "Have you kept

that thing packed all this time?"

She stared at him and nodded. "Yep. You think I'm not always prepared for this? I've been waiting for this break, just like you," she stated, with flint in her tone. She looked from Riff to the others. "He's not going alone, but he would be a fool not to take some backup. This will get ugly fast."

At that, Langdon laughed and stood up. "She's absolutely right. I'm coming too."

Riff glared at him now.

Langdon shook his head, giving Riff a wry smile. "If you think I give a shit about that look on your face, you've got another think coming. I'm not coming alone either." He turned to face Royce.

Royce nodded. "Yep, sounds like a good deal to me."

"No good deal about this," Riff declared in a grating tone. "We might not even have any real information, so this could be yet another dead end." Everyone shook their heads, and Angela glared right at him. Riff groaned, clearly exasperated. "You should wait and see if something is here," Riff added.

"Royce and Langdon will be your backup, Riff. They can help, along with Angela." At that, Terkel got up, handed Riff a phone number, and added in a calm tone, "The original guy you spoke with, the one who supposedly knew something about Sadie's murder but wouldn't talk to you, was just taken out in prison. One of his former cellmates wants to talk. He thinks his life is also in danger, and he has information—but only if we can keep him alive."

"How long do we have to keep him alive?" Riff asked, giving Terk a hard glance. "If this asshole had information I needed five years ago, I won't be all that interested in keeping him alive now."

"I get that," Terkel said. "However, the reality is, without him, it could be another five years before you find someone else willing to talk, so be careful what you wish for. Go talk to him and see if the intel he has is worth making a deal over. If you can get the information, that's up to you what you give him in return."

"Riff may have lost some of his sensibilities over all this," Angela noted, her tone hard, "but I have not. If there is any way to make a deal, we'll make a deal. I won't risk the chance of some slime ball like this dying just because he didn't talk to us years ago. As you all know, there are plenty of situations where people don't want to give up information yet do, usually based on their own survival." Riff turned and opened his mouth to say something, but she stepped up in his face. "No."

Such force was behind that single word that Riff slowly closed his mouth and rolled his eyes. He knew she wouldn't budge, so he just turned back to Terkel. "If you want to send somebody to keep an eye on her, that might be a good idea. Just a heads-up, *I* might be the only one threatening her, but I'll leave her safety in your capable hands. Plus, presumably, you guys have had all the babies you'll want for right now," he quipped, raising an eyebrow. "So maybe you'll decide you don't need Angela's services anymore here at the castle."

At that, Clary laughed. "Nice try," she replied, "but we also know how important she is to you, no matter what you say. We'll confirm that she's safe though." When Riff stared at Clary, she shrugged. "Energy doesn't lie."

He glared at her. "Maybe you shouldn't look."

"Maybe you shouldn't send out such a smokescreen of energy to make the rest of us so very suspicious," she suggested, giving him a warning look. "Remember where you live."

"How could I forget?" he muttered, as he looked around the room, his irritation barely contained.

"If you want to move out, there are easier places to live," Terkel noted, with a smile, "but probably none quite so rewarding."

Riff groaned. "Fine, send somebody to look after her, but everybody better stay the hell out of my way. I don't need anyone to babysit me."

"The two of us can stay out of your way just fine," Langdon confirmed, with a knowing smile shared with Royce, "but the reality is that Angela's focus will involve getting in your way while helping."

"Yeah, *all* of you will be in my way," Riff complained in disgust and then turned to Terk. "You know I work better alone."

Terkel nodded. "You may, but no ditching her. The last thing I need is our energies divided because somebody's got a problem with somebody else," Terk pointed out. "You know I don't tolerate that."

"You already know I have a problem with her," he muttered, as he walked out to the vehicle, Terkel at his side.

"As Clary mentioned, we all know why."

Riff froze at that and frowned at him. "You guys have made that comment several times now, as if you think something is between us. The only thing between us is … her dead sister," he stated harshly. "That makes it pretty crowded, so no room for anything else."

"I get that," Terkel replied. "No room because it's so full of your fiancée and your questions about everything that happened around her death. … Underneath it all is something you will have time to sort out after all this is solved.

Just another reason to get it all dealt with."

"Getting it dealt with is one thing," Riff grumbled, "but replacing Sadie? … That's just not happening." With that, he hopped into the truck, impatiently waiting for Angela to get into the passenger seat, while Langdon and Royce got into another vehicle. Riff turned to Terkel. "If you find anything else …"

"We're on it, and we'll promptly share anything we discover," he replied, "and the guys will be tracking you."

"Hopefully this asshole informant can't get away from us this time."

"Only if he's dead," Terkel said, "hence the need for speed."

"Do you think he's in real danger?" Riff asked, as he turned on the engine and stared at his friend.

"I know he is because your fiancée's killer is desperate to confirm nobody is left alive to tell the tale."

ANGELA STAYED QUIET for the first part of the journey, until she couldn't stand it anymore. "I loved her too, you know?" she muttered.

Riff glanced at her and nodded. "I know you did," he said, his tone flat. "You were also jealous as hell of her."

"If you say so," she muttered. "Not sure *jealousy* is the right word."

"Doesn't really matter now, does it?" he snapped in clipped tone. "Sometimes things just don't work out. You had just broken up with your boyfriend, and you were very jealous of what she and I had."

"Wow," she said, frowning at him. "Where the hell did

you get that from?"

He glanced at her, one eyebrow raised, and added in the same hard tone, "Sadie told me."

Angela let out a gasp. "Jesus, it would have been nice if you'd told me that sooner. I would have completely dispelled that idea for you. Hell no, I wasn't jealous of you two. As for my boyfriend? Yes, he was a louse, and he cheated on me left, right, and center. That was not something I wanted to advertise, so that part I kept to myself. My sister and I definitely had some issues, as many sisters do," she clarified, "particularly toward the end there."

"Yeah, and that was because of that louse of a boyfriend of yours," he stated flatly.

She swallowed a retort that was dying to burst from her lips. "Glad you got it all figured out. So you don't need me to tell you anything about my sister and me, do you?"

"God no," he muttered. "And it's not news when sisters are jealous or have problems with each other forever."

"Maybe not," she conceded. "Yet we were still sisters, and we still loved each other."

He didn't say anything for a moment, then gave a quick nod. "I know that she loved you very much," he replied in a soft tone.

"Yeah? Did she tell you that?" she asked, struggling to keep the cynicism out of her tone—and failing obviously, as he glared at her. "We definitely still had some issues."

"You shouldn't have had any issues, period. Just because your relationship with that guy didn't work out doesn't mean you couldn't have found somebody else," he stated harshly.

"Yeah? I guess your relationship was perfect, wasn't it?"

"No, it wasn't perfect, and, toward the end, something

was going on with her. I never figured it out and still wish I knew what it was." She bit her bottom lip to keep the words back, which he saw right away. He turned to her, immediately skeptical. "Do you know what it was?"

"I might have some ideas," she replied cautiously, "but I'm not prepared to say anything about it right now."

He glared at her. "You know how that secrecy shit pisses me off, right?"

"You can be as pissed off as you want," she said. "I'm well used to it by now."

"What does that mean?" he snapped. He quickly changed lanes and hit the highway. Checking his rearview mirror, sure enough, Langdon and Royce were still behind him. "We don't really need anybody with us, you know? We'll just talk to a prisoner."

"I hear you," she said in that calm tone she used with troublesome patients. Riff was the epitome of troublesome and took it to a whole other level. He'd been a pain in her butt for a very long time, for myriad reasons, but mostly because she'd loved him since what seemed like forever.

She knew the women at Terkel's place understood—or at least recognized the energy, whether Angela's failure to keep her love for Riff a secret or his ability to remain blind to any such thing around him. She would go with the latter. He didn't say anything for a long time, and she wondered if the entire journey would be made in silence. Then she remembered the file. "I want to see the file."

He shrugged. "I emailed it to you."

She frowned at him. "When?"

"Just before we left," he stated. "I figured you would hound me for it anyway."

"Yeah, I probably would," she agreed, pulling out her

phone and downloading the little bit there.

He added, "You know most of it already."

"Yeah, I do, but I haven't had anything to refer back to, you know, to keep it somewhat in my head," she explained. "And facts can get confused or distorted over time."

"Which is my problem with talking to this guy. I mean, after five years, how much of it is he just making up in order to buy himself better accommodations or some other perks?"

"It's possible, but we have to check out every lead, don't we?"

He laughed. "Look at you. You sound as if you're on one of Terkel's missions."

"No," she replied comfortably. "That's not my thing, but it's the same as figuring out problems with any pregnancy or any child. You keep following every trail that shows up, looking for whatever the symptoms point you to. Sometimes you find it. Sometimes you don't."

He didn't say anything to that. "Why did you go into medicine, anyway?" he asked.

He sounded quite genuine, and such puzzlement filled his tone that she burst out laughing. "You do know that doctors are needed, right? Besides, they hold a respectable position in life," she added, with a shrug. "I get that, to you, it's something completely foreign and an odd choice for someone to make."

"It seems strange to me," he stated, with a shrug, "and I know Sadie didn't understand it either."

At that, Angela fell silent and then nodded. "You're right about that. Sadie didn't get it, not at all. She didn't understand. … I don't think she understood anything about it, but my profession wasn't necessarily the problem with us." She looked out the window. "I just needed acceptance, support for my life choices."

"Did you give her support for hers?" he asked, with a note of amusement.

"Considering her life choice was marrying you, and she happily planned on having babies, which supported my own profession, it didn't seem to require much support on my part. It's not as if she needed a college education to be a wife and mom. She never made any attempt to get further education. Yet it was one of the things that she threw back at me a lot. She didn't see the point in racking up all that student debt. She thought college was useless."

"What?" he asked, startled.

Angela stared out the window, knowing that it wasn't fair to bring up her dead sister's words or to dredge up the past at all, but her sister and her words still had the power to hurt Angela. So, anything that still had the power to hurt her was something she was desperately trying to work on. "She told me that I would forever work, needing a good job to pay off those student loans because I would never have a good man," she shared finally.

He gave a bark of laughter. "What does one have to do with the other?"

Surprised, she frowned at him. She sure as hell didn't expect that response. "Most people would understand that a *good man*, … at least in Sadie's world, meant the good man's wife would not have to work. So, a good job was something I needed to care about because I couldn't have a good man to bring in enough money."

He was very quiet for a long time. "I'd forgotten how much money mattered to her."

"Yeah, money, status, things, … all of that mattered to her. You did know that, right?"

"Sure, I did," he said, with a shrug, "but I loved her, so I was willing to live with it."

"Of course," she whispered. "And, because you were willing to live with it, she got what she wanted. Whereas I didn't want to be dependent on a man to support me. I wanted to feel useful and to contribute to the world around me. Plus, I love children."

"Yet you have none of your own."

"Wow, … are you channeling that mocking tone right from Sadie?"

"No," he said. "Nothing like that. I just wondered if there was a reason."

"A couple of them," she muttered, still bitter about the slight. "One, I'm not sure I can have any. Two, in my world, they require more than just a sire. I would prefer to have children where the father is permanently around to raise them with me. Since I haven't found a decent man, I need to decide if any of that still matters."

By the expression on his face, Angela noted this revelation was a surprise for Riff.

"I deal with babies on a day-to-day basis, and sometimes that's enough." she explained. "Sometimes I think I would be crazy to even go in that direction."

Riff frowned. "I guess if you're thinking you can't have any children, you've already done a bunch of tests."

He sounded sympathetic, almost apologetic, and nothing like himself. Angela frowned.

Riff continued. "That's got to be traumatizing in itself, being around babies all the time, the way you are."

"I guess a lot of people would think that, but it's not about *being around babies*. It's about helping them, helping the mothers, and helping both have the life they want.

Motherhood isn't just about getting pregnant and popping out a baby. I mean, that's the pregnancy part, but so much more goes into it afterward, and so many things can go wrong with these organic bodies of ours.

"Sometimes it's hard when you tell a woman that her child's got a disease or a physical ailment before it's even born. Then afterward you follow up and spend years trying to get the child proper treatment, while offering support to the mother who's slowly having a breakdown because her child will never be normal. Sometimes divorces happen, and sometimes there's no money for medical help, and sometimes people come to the point where occasionally bad things happen."

He glanced over at her, frowning.

She stared out the window, trying not to see the look on his face.

"That sounds as if something's just happened. What's going on?"

"Not just now," she clarified, "but a few months back. I became quite close to a woman, after she gave birth to three healthy boys over three years, but she really, … like desperately, wanted a daughter. When her daughter was born with severe physical and mental disabilities, she managed for about a year and a half, but what none of us saw was the deterioration on the inside. Then one day she broke— mentally—and, when her husband was at work, she took his pistol, shot all four kids, then shot herself. … There's just no coming back from that."

"Jesus," Riff muttered. "Why kill the healthy children?"

"Why kill any children?" she asked sharply.

He winced. "You're right, my mistake, but, if she's struggling with what's happening with the child who has so many problems, you would like to think that she could have seen a way to give the healthy children a better life."

Angela sighed. "A lot of times they think that the sickly children are better off dead. She was heading for a divorce, possibly wanted to preserve the status quo, and didn't want the kids to find out, didn't want the kids to go through the pain of a divorce. I don't know. It's not as if she talked to me about it or anything." At that, she winced. "Sorry, I didn't mean that to come across like she should have or that I blame her for it."

"But you do, don't you?"

She hesitated, then replied, "Blame is a very strong thing. I wish she had talked to me about it, sure, and I did ask her to get help at one point in time. Yet I didn't force it. At no time did I think she was suicidal—or worse. I mean, that's not what I was thinking about her status at all. I was trying to get her funding for a new home, where she could be with the kids full time, but we didn't get that far," she noted in a hoarse voice. "There just wasn't enough time before she decided to do this. Anyway, that's enough heart-to-heart for now about a very depressing topic."

"Christ, you're not kidding," he agreed. "I guess you must think my obsession with Sadie's murder is trivial when compared to that."

"The trouble is, I live and work with these stories," she stated, turning to him. "Meanwhile, you've got your own problems. If I asked you to go get help, I know I would get the exact same answer that I get from a lot of my patients, so I don't even bother. Yet talking to someone could really do you some good."

He laughed. "Thanks, but I don't need it."

"Nobody ever thinks they need help or that the help will

do anything for them," she explained, with a wry smile. "I get that. I do, but sometimes? … It would be awfully nice if people would listen."

"Yeah? And, if somebody told you to get help, would you?"

She faced him. "I did actually. Right after Sadie's murder." She paused at the word, knowing that there was a certain amount of freedom in being able to say it now, and that was progress because, for the longest time, she couldn't even begin to acknowledge it. "After her murder, I knew I needed help," she acknowledged in a faint voice. "I couldn't give my patients the best of me when there wasn't any *best of me* left. I was grieving. I felt horribly guilty, as if I should have been there for her, should have somehow been able to stop this," she shared, with a headshake.

Angela sighed. "Yet the fact is, I couldn't. I didn't even know it was happening, wouldn't have known how to prevent it if I had known, but that doesn't stop me from thinking that way. What if I'd been there that day? What if we hadn't had a fight a few weeks earlier? What if I had gone to visit her that day instead? Maybe it wouldn't have happened."

"Or maybe both of you would have been murdered," he declared, his tone pensive. "I hadn't realized that you felt guilty."

"I think that just is part and parcel when a loved one is murdered," she began. "Everybody feels guilty because, no matter which way you look at it, an endless set of *what ifs* follow. You don't know why it happened. You don't know the details, outside of the actual death. You don't know whether she stopped in to see somebody, it was completely random, or she pissed off somebody. You don't just know.

So then you can't stop thinking *What if I'd been there that day? What if I'd visited her that day? Why did I work all the time? Why didn't I do more with her?*"

"You guys did a lot together," he noted, "until whatever that blowup was. So I guess that goes along with it, *huh?*"

"To a certain extent," she said carefully. "I'm hoping that solving this will bring closure, not so much about the guilt anymore. This current lead, right now, is a way to move on. Yet I have done so in many, many ways. I mean, that's what going to see a therapist was all about for me. I needed a counselor to help me find a way past that guilt of not having been there for her—and for not having been the one who was murdered. Survivor's guilt is a horrible thing."

"Yeah, I've heard that before," he replied, "though I can't say I've ever dealt with it."

"That's because you're not dealing," she pointed out softly. "All you can think about is revenge."

"Are you so sure it's revenge?" he asked, looking over at her.

"You tell me. If it isn't revenge, then what is it?"

"Closure, answers, justice, a chance to say goodbye."

"Yeah, that's something we would all have liked, isn't it? I don't think any of us realize, when you say goodbye in the morning, how you may not see somebody again at the end of the day," she muttered. "That's one of the hardest things."

"It is," he conceded. "I wasn't even in the country at the time."

"No, you were off on one of your lovely missions." She snorted.

"Did Sadie have a problem with that?" he asked her quietly.

She had been watching the countryside to see how close

they were to the end of their journey. She took her attention off that once she realized he was serious. "I don't know that she ever did. I think she missed you and kept busy while you were away." It was really important for Angela to keep her tone of voice just right, to carefully choose her words. Still, his gaze was searching as he eyed her. "Keep your focus on the road," she said in exasperation.

"You're not telling me something. If there's one thing that really pisses me off," he spat, his tone low and hard, "it's when people keep information from me."

"That's nice," she replied. "Isn't that our turnoff up there?"

He made the turn, and they watched in the rearview mirror as the rest of the team came up behind them. As they reached the security area for the prison, he asked her in a curious tone, "You ever been in here?"

"No, not exactly my kind of place."

"Yet you're an attractive woman, about to walk into a place where men don't get to see much in the way of women, so don't be upset at the comments."

She laughed. "I may work mostly with women, but along with that comes an awful lot of contact with really *assholey* husbands," she declared. "So I'm not too bothered about seeing the worst of the males in here. I suspect it's just a sampling of what every normal society has anyway. You would be surprised at the shit that happens with the husbands sometimes."

And, with that, she hopped out, slammed the door, and waited for the others to join her.

CHAPTER 2

GETTING THROUGH PRISON security was an interesting process. Angela followed instructions, kept herself positioned between the three men, surprised that all four of them would be allowed in. However, when it came down to the actual interview room, they were told that only two could go in. She immediately stepped up. "I'm going." When Riff glared at her, she shrugged. "I think you should come with me."

"I was planning on it," he stated, "but I would take one of the guys with me."

"That sounds nice and all," she began, giving them all a mock-apologetic look, "but it's not happening." Without even looking back, she stepped into the room, knowing that Riff would be right behind her.

The prisoner was there, and she remembered from the file that his name was James. James Teespawl. In prison, he went by Tee most of the time. That was supposed to be some sort of egotistic selection, so they could feel bigger, better, … badder somehow. She didn't know a lot about how that worked in a prison environment. She couldn't even begin to understand that whole psychology element when used here. As she studied Teespawl, she saw nothing but a lanky, wiry man, who looked more afraid than she expected, yet hopeful in a way.

Maybe the thought of seeing a woman made him hopeful because his expression changed when Riff stepped into the room behind her, and Teespawl fidgeted uneasily. That was nothing new, Riff had that same effect on a lot of people. She seemed to be among the few people who were immune to him, but then it wasn't even immunity. It was something completely different, and she knew it.

She smiled at Teespawl. "May I call you James?" He hesitated and then finally nodded. "I suppose nobody but your mom calls you that," she added.

He flushed and nodded. "You got that night. … Thankfully she passed on a couple years back."

"Ah, so she doesn't know that you're in here?"

He shook his head. "She did know unfortunately. My court case was coming up, but she knew in her heart of hearts that I would go free and that she would live to see it," he added, with another headshake. "She died before we got through everything. That just made it all kinds of hard."

"Of course it did, but then, when the verdict came through, you were probably glad she wasn't here for that."

He winced. "What are you doing here?" he asked, glaring at her, obviously not liking where this conversation was going.

"The woman we want the information on," she stated, "was my sister."

"Oh," he muttered, staring down at his hands.

"So, the question is whether you have something valuable to tell us," she pointed out, continuing to do the talking, knowing that Riff would jump in anytime he didn't like her approach. "Or is this just an excuse to make your world easier?"

He glared at her. "You've got no call to say that to me."

"Maybe not," she conceded, "but there were an awful lot of closed mouths at the time."

He nodded. "Yeah, and now a couple of those mouths have been closed forever," he snapped in a warning tone. "So that information is getting harder and harder to come by."

"I'm sure it is," she agreed, nodding. "The question is, why do you want to share it anyway? Why now?"

He looked over at the guard, then at her. "Because I don't want to be next."

"*Right*," Riff muttered, his tone hard.

"So essentially we can help each other." James looked at Riff nervously and nodded. "That's the way I figured it. I mean, … I help you, and you help me. Right?"

"What is it that you have that'll help us?" she asked curiously.

"I need to know what you can do to help me first."

"I guess it depends on how much information you even have," she replied, with half a laugh. "Then the next part would be whether it's of any interest to the government or not."

At that, his mouth dropped. "What difference does it make if it's of any help to the government?"

Angela shrugged. "The reality is, we can only do so much. However, if you have anything that would help the government solve this murder, … they can do a whole lot more than we can."

He frowned at her, then over at Riff. "I don't know anything about the government," he said in confusion. "It was just information about that woman."

"Let's start with that then. What woman?" Riff asked. "What do you know about it?"

"Her name was Sadie Carson," James said, "and she was

murdered a few years back."

Riff asked, "Did you have anything to do with it?"

"No, no, hell no," James replied, with a hurried shake of his head. "I didn't have anything to do with it, but my cellmate told me about it. Then, soon afterward, he ended up dying. Like … very soon after," he clarified, looking around nervously. He lowered his voice. "It happened so quick. I wouldn't be shocked if one of the guards didn't have something to do with it."

The guard in the back of the room rolled his eyes.

Angela smiled at the guard. "I guess you hear that a lot, don't you?"

The guard nodded. "Yeah, I sure do. These guys will do anything to avoid facing reality."

At that, James glared at him, his tone hard as he added, "I didn't say *you* might have, but you know some of the guards in here are no good."

The guard relaxed at that. "You're just talking BS." Then he fell quiet and looked over at Riff. "Hurry up and do your talking. You don't have all day."

Angela grimaced. Not having all day really meant that they didn't have a whole lot of time at all. "So, what did this cellmate tell you?" she asked James, leaning in slightly. "If it's good information, we'll see what we can do about your … situation."

"No, no, no, no," James sputtered. "You need to tell me what you can do for me first because the information I've got is good. I swear."

"I hope it's good," Riff replied, "because, if it isn't, we came a long way for nothing." His tone oozed frustration, and anyone who heard it felt some level of fear. At that, James swallowed nervously, looked at her again, and asked,

"You can make this happen, can't you?"

"What is it you want to happen?" she asked. Not wanting to lie, she added, "We can certainly advocate on your behalf if you've got information that's helpful, but the information must actually be helpful."

"I need out of here," James stated, lowering his voice. "They killed my cellmate while he was here in prison, so somebody in here is keeping track of this shit."

"Maybe so," she acknowledged, "but why would anybody care?"

"Because he knew who done it," James whispered.

"This cellmate of yours, did he tell you who did it?" Angela asked.

He looked as if he wanted to say yes, but he shook his head. "He didn't give a name."

"Of course not," she muttered, staring at him with disappointment. "If he didn't give you the name, then what did he tell you?"

"He told me how it all went down, and he gave me an idea of who it was. And you better believe me when I say that guy is dangerous as hell, like tied to the mob or something." He shuddered visibly at his own words.

Riff interjected, "Mob? Unlikely. I want to know why she was murdered. I don't understand how anybody could have anything against her."

James hesitated. "There was some talk about that. I guess it was somebody she was close to."

At that, Riff stiffened. "You mean, the murder was done by somebody close to her or the reason for the murder was because of somebody close to her?"

James shook his head and shrugged. "I just heard it involved somebody close to her. Someone was angry. I'm not sure if it was in retaliation for somebody close to her or what. It was so long ago, but that is just my idea."

"Why don't you just tell us what you know," Riff snapped impatiently. "Stop all the innuendos about knowing something you don't really know anything about."

At that, James glared at him. "I've got to confirm I get something for it."

"How about your life?" Riff asked in a threatening tone. "Isn't that worth something?"

"Sure, it is," James confirmed, "but, so far, you guys aren't talking game."

"So, you want to change prisons and what else?" she asked, trying to placate the situation because this was going nowhere.

"I want a change of prison, and I want my sentence commuted."

Riff laughed. "That's not happening, no matter what you tell me. Forget that. Commuted sentence is completely off the table."

James settled back and glared at him.

"You know that's not within anybody's ability but the government's, right?" she asked. "Don't even try telling me you don't know that."

He groaned. "Fine, get me into a safer prison, away from whatever the hell's going on here."

Angela shook her head. "And yet, if this prison really has that kind of scenario happening here, you won't be safe in another prison either. Maybe for a while but not for long."

James' shoulders slumped. "I know," he muttered. "I worry about that. I've got five more years, and I was really hoping to get those commuted."

"If you go to a smaller prison somewhere out in the

boondocks for those years, you would hopefully get through it," she suggested. "Take a chance."

James nodded. "That's the plan anyway, if you can do that much." James's gaze went from Riff to her.

She shrugged and added, "What I can tell you is that we'll try."

Riff stared at her, back at the prisoner, and nodded. "We can try."

James took a deep breath. "Fine. What I can tell you is that she went to meet somebody that night, and the guy she went to meet was in trouble. He had some enemies back then, hounding him about some smuggling and shit. I heard he'd taken money that was supposed to go to somebody else and kept it," he shared. "So someone came to kill him, and that's when she got killed too. She was in the wrong place at the wrong time."

Riff asked, his tone hard, "What do you mean by *meeting him?*"

James gave Riff a dour expression. "She met him in a motel, so what do you think?"

"But her body was found on an overpass," Angela stated because she felt Riff about to blow a fuse. "What's this about a motel?"

"She was moved, wasn't she?" James asked.

Angela nodded. "Yes, that is quite true. The overpass wasn't the actual kill spot, but we never did find out where it happened."

"I can tell you the name of the motel and the general area where one of those motels were," James replied. "Outside of that, I don't have a whole lot more to give you."

Riff sat back and stared at James. She studied Riff's face for a quick moment and then shifted back to the prisoner.

"Give us the name of the motel, and we'll see if it's really the crime scene. Then we'll get back to you."

James hesitated but realized he didn't have a whole lot of choice in the matter, especially not with the guard now pointing to his watch. "The Last Chance Motel in a small town on the outskirts of London."

She nodded. "That's not too far of a drive from here."

"No," James replied.

Angela asked, "How often did they meet?"

He looked at her and shrugged. "I don't know how often, but it wasn't the first time. My cellmate told me that much."

She gave him a clipped nod. Riff looked at her sideways, and there was that same cold, calculated fury that she'd gotten so used to. For her, hearing about Sadie at some seedy motel with another man wasn't exactly news, but Angela knew Riff would really be struggling with it. She turned to James and asked, "This dead guy, who made all these enemies, what was his name?"

"Johnny Waco," James replied reluctantly.

"And the name of your dead cellmate?" she asked.

"He was Johnny Waco's brother."

She stopped to stare at James.

He nodded slowly. "Yeah, that's how I found out."

Knowing that this interrogation would end very quickly, she nodded and wrote down her phone number and Riff's on a piece of paper and handed it to James. "Here's our phone numbers. For us to do very much, we need every single detail we can possibly get on this. So, if you come up with anything else, anything you can think of, you must tell us. Like, who Johnny was in trouble with, any names you can associate with him, what he was doing to get himself arrested to begin with, all of it. You need to help us if you want us to help you."

"All I know is that Chip was involved somehow. I don't know anything about Chip, but I know you can find him in that same area as the motel," James added, as he stood and pocketed the phone numbers. He looked over at her. "You won't forget where you got the information, right?"

Such anxiety filled his tone that she nodded. "We won't forget."

And, with that, James was led out of the interrogation room.

She quickly hustled Riff out of the room. Even though it appeared he was walking and acting completely normal, that wasn't the case at all. The two men waiting for them in a nearby hallway fell in line but were silent. Riff's energy was all too easy to read.

Outside the prisoner area but still not out of the building, the foursome came upon a large entranceway, where Riff grabbed Angela by the arm and pulled her around, glaring at her while ignoring the other two.

She was surprised that he'd managed to keep it together even this long, but she still just waited for the inevitable.

"What the hell was that all about?" he asked with such force that it even rattled her for a moment.

She stared up at him. "What was what all about?"

He narrowed his gaze. "I'm not a fool. Why were you even bargaining with that liar?"

She winced. She knew Riff could go either way on this one, but of course he chose not to believe anything James said. "How do you know that he's lying?" she asked.

"Because she was my fiancée, and the one thing I do know is that she didn't step out on me. Plus *the mob*? Really?

Can you see Sadie knowing *the mob*?"

Angela turned and looked around the main entrance area. "Can we get out of here? We will talk outside." When he grabbed her by the arm again, she looked up at him and retorted, "And I mean it. We'll talk outside. And I can walk on my own, so thanks."

He held his peace until they got outside, where he turned her around and snapped, "Talk to me."

Langdon and Royce froze, their gazes going from one to the other.

RIFF SEARCHED ANGELA'S face, looking for something that confirmed she didn't know anything about Sadie running around on him and most definitely not with the mob. But he reared back in shock as he stared at her. "You believe that asshole?" Her expression revealed that he was completely lost in disbelief.

She winced. "Yeah, in many ways I do," she stated flatly.

Langdon and Royce approached them, and Riff glared at Angela for good measure, before addressing the men. "So, we have a motel where Sadie was apparently murdered, and we have the name of the guy she was with."

Angela nodded, while holding up her index finger. "Somebody named Chip was also involved in the whole scenario," she quickly explained. "We'll head over to the motel right now and see if we can confirm that it was the crime scene and not just the ramblings of a criminal desperate to get out of his sentence."

"We're coming with you," Royce replied, his gaze steady on Riff.

She nodded. "This time I'm driving."

"You are not driving," Riff bit off.

"If you don't get a hold of yourself," she snapped, as the others walked over to their vehicle, "I will be driving because I can't trust you behind the wheel right now."

"I'm driving," he repeated, giving her no argument.

She hesitated but let him get in the driver's seat. There, he turned on the engine, trying to figure out how to even begin to process the information that she seemed so ready to believe.

"Why?" he bit off. "Why do you believe this guy?"

"Because I knew she was having an affair," she stated in a calm, collected tone, inwardly wincing at the blow to come.

He cranked the steering wheel hard, pulling out onto the road, sending her ever-so-slightly against the far door. His anger bloomed inside, a fury he didn't even recognize, and he shook his head. "No," he snapped.

"Yes," she countered.

He turned several times to look at her, questions rapidly formulating in his brain, only to die before they ever made it into words. He kept shaking his head. "No."

As soon as he would say no, she would say yes.

"Proof?" he asked.

"Oh, I have proof," she muttered, "but you won't like it."

"Why would you not have told me about this before? I mean, if it's true—and I'm not saying it is—but if it were true, you would have told me. It would have had huge repercussions on the initial investigation into her death."

"Not when she was supposedly randomly attacked and killed on an overpass, not when she was supposed to be home that night. It wouldn't have made any difference," she countered.

"That's not true, and I don't believe you."

"You don't believe me because you don't want to," she snapped, "and you don't want to dare even look because, in your mind, you already know." He snorted at that. "That's one of the reasons you find it so hard to pinpoint who killed her," she added. "All because you knew she wasn't faithful and a part of you feels guilty because you just let it go on. You didn't want to confront her and to destroy your little happy bubble."

"What the hell are you talking about?" he roared. He smacked his fist against the steering wheel but didn't trust himself to look at her.

"You knew," she repeated. "You may not have understood just what was going on, but you knew something was wrong," she snapped again. "If I saw it, no way you didn't."

He felt himself quaking inside, but he had absolutely no way to even consider what she was saying because everything just came back as this red haze. He shook his head. "I would have done something about it, if I had known," he declared. "That's hardly something I would just let her do, not without putting a stop to it."

"It's not that easy because, if you put a stop to it, that meant you had to acknowledge that she was doing it in the first place," Angela retorted, "and that's something you weren't prepared to consider back then, much less now."

"That is bullshit," Riff spat. "Do I look like somebody who would allow her to do that?"

"You knew that, if you did acknowledge it, it would change everything for you. You would have to acknowledge that your fiancée was cheating on you. You would have to acknowledge that every time you went out of town, you had no idea what she was doing, nor who she was doing it with.

Above all, you would have to acknowledge that this woman you absolutely adored, loved, and *trusted*," she hesitated and then plundered forward, "didn't adore you back. And didn't love you enough to be faithful."

CHAPTER 3

ANGELA KNEW THERE would be no easy way to tell Riff, and he had been silent ever since. Still, her method had been rather brutal, and she couldn't take back the words. Yet she didn't really want to take them back. She knew what her sister had been like all along, but obviously Riff hadn't come to the point where he could accept it. Angela didn't blame him, It was a rude awakening and hard to realize that your engagement was a lie, a lie that her sister had perpetrated.

Riff pulled up to the front of the target motel, where the murder supposedly happened. He just glared at her as they got out. "We'll discuss it later."

She didn't say anything because, of course, they would discuss it later. They would hash it out, time and time again, because they could do nothing else, not until Riff finally came to terms with it.

As they walked into the motel, she noted, "You realize it's been five years, and they won't likely know anything."

"Yeah, I know that," he snapped, biting off her head. Inside the motel, he asked to speak with the manager.

The woman eyed them quizzically. "I am the manager."

He smiled. "Are you also the owner?"

She nodded. "I am."

"How long have you owned this space?"

She narrowed her gaze at him. "About twenty years. Why?"

Pulling out a picture of Sadie, he held it up so she could see it. "About five years ago, this woman came here for a night."

She frowned at him and then laughed. "You expect me to remember somebody from five years ago?" she asked.

"It would be helpful if you could remember," Angela stated. "She was murdered, and we just found out that she was murdered here."

The owner stared at her in shock. "Good God, how the hell would I have any idea if that's what happened?"

"I guess it depends on whether you found an inordinate amount of blood somewhere," Riff pointed out. "Any unusual damage or something of that nature."

"You mean, a crime scene?" she muttered in shock. "You think I wouldn't have called the cops?" When they just stared at her, the owner took a deep breath. "I get it. I do know that this motel is often used for clandestine meetups," she conceded, "but that's not my fault. I would love to raise our clientele to host people with a little more class, but that's pretty hard to do in this town," she noted in exasperation. "I came to terms with what *often* goes on here a long time ago, but I can tell you flat-out that I can't recall ever having witnessed anything even close to what you've described."

"So, at no point in time did bedding go missing?" Angela asked.

At that, the owner turned to her and frowned. "Why would you say that?"

"Because, if she'd been killed—say, on the bed—then the bedding would be a dead giveaway. So the killer would dispose of the sheets and the bedspread."

"Sure, but wouldn't there be blood everywhere else?" she asked.

Angela shrugged. "Not if they flipped the mattress. How often do you flip mattresses here?"

The owner winced and shook her head. "We don't."

"Right. We also have the name of the person who would have met her here. Johnny Waco."

The owner nodded. "He used to come here quite a bit," she acknowledged, as she scrunched up her nose in distaste. She again focused on the picture of Sadie and tapped it. "It could have been her, though I can't be sure. I did see her but not for very long."

"Would she have come just once or twice, maybe more?" Angela asked.

"Oh, it was definitely a few times at least," the owner murmured. "I don't know when I saw her last. Come to think of it, I haven't seen Waco for a long time either."

Angela nodded. "He's dead too."

The owner winced at that. "That's no surprise. He was the type." She groaned. "I do remember he always asked for one specific room though."

"Why that one room?" Angela asked.

"He just said it was the easiest to defend."

At that, Riff stiffened. "Did he say from what?"

"He used to joke about angry husbands, pissed-off partners, something along that line. He always treated life as if it were a joke, just a merry-go-round that you were on for a while, and then you got off. I always suspected he would cash in his chips way earlier than everybody else in this life, and it sounds as if I was right." The owner turned, grabbed a set of keys, and announced, "I can show you the room that he used, but I'm telling you that it was years ago."

"Yeah, it would have been five years ago. Did you change out the mattresses in the meantime?" Angela asked.

The owner gave her a skeptical smile. "Do I look as if I have money to change out the mattresses?"

"It seems you're not doing too badly here," she murmured.

"You're right. We're doing better now than we ever have before—by quite a bit. The new highway made a big difference, and I had the exterior of the property painted," she shared. "So you're right, but new mattresses aren't on the agenda just yet. I would love to do some interior painting, some new decorating, all in an attempt to get repeat customers—and not the kind that Johnny and his lady friends were."

"Lady friends, plural?" Angela clarified.

"Yeah, Johnny always kept multiples," the owner added. "He tended to stick with one for a while, but then he would switch it up. He had a lot of women here over the years. I gave him a special rate," she admitted, with a wink, "which kept him coming back for more."

Angela asked, "Were they always married women?"

The owner shrugged, shaking her head. "Who knows? Believe me that I didn't ask." The whole time the two women were talking, Riff stayed very quiet. When they got to the room in question, the owner pointed out, "You're lucky it's not rented right now. It's popular because it faces the highway."

"Good enough," Angela replied. "Will you give us a few minutes? I know it's unlikely we'll find anything, but we do need to look." The woman stared at her and hesitated. Angela pulled some cash from her pocket and peeled off a fifty.

The owner beamed. "That's almost an hour's worth, so go for it." And, with that, the motel owner walked out.

Angela snorted as the woman closed the door behind her. "Jesus, fifty bucks for an hour? Wow. At that rate, a person could afford to pay for a few hours." She tried to keep her tone light as she looked over at Riff, but he was still in a dark place, whatever that place was. "I'll take a look around," she added and walked into the bathroom.

It was a standard run-of-the-mill cheap motel room, with white fixtures and absolutely no redeeming features, nothing that would encourage Angela to stay. However, if she were a traveler on the road and was tired and worn out, it would do. She checked everything there was to see in the bathroom, but nothing was noteworthy.

As she headed back to the bedroom, she found Riff standing there, staring at the bed. She walked over and carefully lifted off the bedding and the sheets, studying what appeared to be a normal-looking mattress. She sighed as she faced him. "We need to lift this."

He jerked, as if startled, then pinched his lips together, walked closer, and quickly flipped over the mattress. A stunned silence fell over the room.

"Oh, shit," she whispered.

RIFF FOUND IT damn-near impossible to even begin to believe that Angela had given credence to the words of Teespawl, that criminal asshole—lies that would just besmirch his fiancée's reputation and cause all kinds of pain to people who didn't need to go through all that. Riff had held on to that belief, even as he'd listened to the motel owner talk about this Johnny guy, bringing in different women, because Riff knew that did not include his fiancée.

No way Sadie would do such a thing.

He didn't care what Angela said. Yet, after flipping that mattress and staring down at the massive bloodstains, now it became an entirely different story. He quickly pulled out his phone and called Jonas.

"To what do I owe this honor?" Jonas asked in exasperation. "Do you know what time it is?"

"Yes, time to get a crew to the Last Chance Motel." Then he quickly gave him the address.

"And I should give a shit, why?"

"How about an unreported murder?"

A stunned silence came from the other end. "What did you find?" he asked, his tone brisk.

Trying to keep his voice emotionless, Riff detailed what they had discovered so far. "Right now, I'm standing in a room, looking at a heavily stained mattress, and nobody, even after all this time, ever bothered to flip it. Bloodstains are all over it."

"Bloody hell."

Just then a knock came on the door. While Riff continued to speak to Jonas, he turned to watch as Angela opened the door, letting in the two other men on their team, and heard their reactions. "I've got Royce and Langdon here with me right now," Riff told Jonas, "but we'll need a forensics team."

"No problem. It would be good if we did have the original crime scene for Sadie's murder," Jonas noted. "That's been missing this whole time."

"We also need to talk about the lovely criminal who gave us the information. It seems he would want a move to a much better holding cell."

"Sure, he would," Jonas muttered, "and you promised

him everything, didn't you?"

"No, but we did say we would try," Riff clarified. "I've got to go." And, with that, he ended the call and turned to Royce and Langdon.

The men were studying the bloodstain. "That's a lot of blood," Langdon stated.

Riff nodded. "Too much to be ignored. I just called Jonas to send over a forensic team."

"The owner will love that," Langdon muttered, shaking his head. "I'm sure you can imagine her squawking over how much time and money she'll lose because of it."

"Yet she needs to confirm she doesn't do anything to obstruct justice in her establishment because that would have a very negative impact on her business," Angela reminded them.

"Oh, we hear you," Langdon agreed, with a big grin, "but I don't think anybody will really care."

Angela nodded. "They won't, and that's just sad because somebody apparently died here. Even if it's not who we think it was, we need to confirm that somebody is aware of what happened here."

"Now what?" Royce asked.

"I'll take a good look through this place and see if anything is here," Langdon replied, studiously avoiding looking at Riff. Langdon turned to Royce. "You?"

"I'll help. So let's tear apart this place because you know that's what the forensic team will do when they get here."

"Wear gloves," Angela added absentmindedly.

They laughed as they held up their hands, which were already gloved.

She sighed and nodded. "Good. Let's confirm everything is done properly this time."

They nodded with the sober realization that the reason this case hadn't been solved up until now was because of too many screwups, one of which was not finding out that Sadie had apparently been having secret meetings with unsavory people from the criminal world.

And Angela had kept silent too. Why? Riff really wanted answers to that question.

The others continued to ignore Riff and went about tearing apart the place.

As for Riff, he heard all the goings-on around him, but he was lost, adrift in his own world. He heard them talking among themselves and knew they were giving him time and space, but there wouldn't be any time and space that was safe for him, not if this was his fiancée's blood. Chances were, he was about to find out more than he bargained for.

His reactions started to set in, and he clamped down tight on his emotions, even as he felt a small hand slide into his. He squeezed Angela's fingers and croaked, "I'm fine."

"I'm glad you are," she whispered, her voice a little shaky, "because I'm not. Not at all." That served to remind him that this wasn't just about him, and it wasn't just about his dead fiancée. This was also the murder scene for Angela's sister.

CHAPTER 4

ANGELA SWALLOWED ANOTHER sip of hot coffee and kept her face down and turned away from the uncomfortable energy shared by their foursome. They had left the seedy motel and had regrouped around a table in the small coffee shop on the first floor of a proper hotel in London, where they might stay for a while. Both Royce and Langdon appeared to be keeping up a conversation, while Riff just stared at his coffee, and she wasn't doing much better. Finally she lifted her head and looked at the others. "Any suggestions for what we do now?"

Riff raised his gaze to her and reminded her, "We're waiting for Jonas."

"I just won't sit in a hotel forever, even this nice one," she muttered, frowning at him. "How many hours before they get forensic evidence back? We already know it was blood. What we don't know is whether it was my sister's blood."

Langdon interjected, "It'll take some time in order to get that information." Then he shrugged. "We were just discussing how it's probably best to head back home for now," Langdon suggested in a sympathetic tone. "Tomorrow's a new day. Hopefully by morning we'll get more information, and then we'll go from there."

She nodded. "That's a good idea." She looked down at

her watch and winced. "It's seven already."

"We'll still be home in a couple hours," Royce noted. "It's better to go home and come back tomorrow, than stay here and do nothing. Sorry if that comes across as insensitive. That's not my intent."

She nodded. "It's not. What about you?" She turned to Riff.

"I'm staying."

She let out her breath slowly. "Staying where?"

"I don't know yet," he replied, raising his gaze, which was completely unreadable.

"You can't just stay here. This town isn't a memorial, and you can't sort through her life some place where she hasn't been in a very long time. Let's go home, and we can talk on the way."

He hesitated, his gaze searching hers, and then he gave in. "Fine, if you'll finally tell me the truth. The complete truth."

"I'll tell you the truth, but that doesn't mean you'll want to hear it." She glanced at the others, one of whom had an eyebrow raised, hoping she would give them some information. "Let me talk to him first," she replied.

They didn't like it, particularly considering there was now some actual evidence of somebody's murder, but she also knew that she had to get Riff to understand the truth of the matter before this went any further. "Riff and I must talk on the way home, and I'll update you guys when we get there."

They both nodded, and Langdon added, "In that case we're heading home." They hopped up and walked out to their vehicle.

She looked over at Riff. "You want me to drive?"

"No," he snapped.

They got into the vehicle without any more interaction and followed the other two as they headed out, back toward home again. "As days go," she muttered, "this one's been plenty tough."

"Depends on who you're talking to about it," he declared heatedly. "I still can't believe you think all this is true."

"And I can't believe that you don't," she muttered.

"I don't have any proof."

She asked, "If that's her blood on that mattress, will that be proof enough?"

He frowned at her and then quickly focused on the road. "I won't have any choice at that point, will I?"

"No, you probably won't," she agreed, "so let's hope they find the evidence that you need."

He went silent for a very long ten minutes. "You really believe she had affairs?"

"Yes."

"How could you not have told me, if that's true?"

"Listen to yourself. You won't accept it *even now*, when she's been gone all this time," she pointed out in exasperation. "No way you would have talked about this back then. You probably would have—"

"What? Come after you?"

"No, not that."

"You mean, back when I had a chance to get the truth from her?"

"Yes, back when you had a chance to get the truth from her," she confirmed, without making any excuses.

"It doesn't speak all that well for you that you would keep that from me, ... from everyone."

"Really?" she asked, astonished. Then, with a broken laugh, she added, "Why don't you ask me how I know for a fact that she had affairs? Why don't you ask me those questions?"

Warily, he nodded. "Fine, so tell me how you know for sure."

"Because it was my fiancé she was screwing around with," she snapped. "That's how I knew for sure." She glared at him. "Believe me that my fiancé was not the first, but that is the reason we broke up and is also the reason that my beloved sister and I fought so heavily." Riff's breath let out in a *whoosh*, and she nodded. "Yeah, you damn-well better believe it," she snapped.

"I found them together in bed, so there was absolutely no doubt what they were doing. Something else you'll want to know is that Sadie laughed. She thought it was great fun and told me that it was high time I found out the truth about them. He was angry when he heard that, explaining how Sadie had been after him for months and months. Finally he gave in at a weak moment, or so he said. To Sadie, it was a quick roll in the hay that meant absolutely nothing to her. That may well have been true, but, to me, it meant everything," she declared, feeling the same pain when she had found them together.

"There is no betrayal like one that comes from your own damn family," she muttered.

He hesitated, then asked, "Why didn't you tell me?"

"At the time, I was still too traumatized to figure out what I was doing myself. Believe me that you weren't exactly at the top of my list of things to deal with, and that's only *part* of what my sister had to say to me that day," she stated, followed by a brutal laugh. "She let me have an awful lot of truths that I really didn't need or want, and her words still sting to this day," she admitted.

Angela continued. "So, don't think I'll be letting you off the hook on any of this, though it's not a picnic even telling you about all of it because Sadie made it very clear what she thought of me. The fact that she died soon afterward meant that I've had to carry those words in my head all this time. It's also why I didn't mention it at the time. My ex was traveling when she was murdered, so he didn't do it. I had no idea someone else was in her life."

She was trying to hold back the tears. "Those are the thoughts and the images and the memories I get to keep," she declared, her tone washed in bitterness. "And that's not easy, having ugly memories instead of all the beautiful ones I'd had before. Instead, I see Sadie for who she really was— the spoiled, pampered little bitch who did absolutely nothing for anybody else, taking whatever she wanted and treating everything in life as a big joke. You can't even say that she had a fun-loving, over-the-top sense of humor. She was purely arrogant and selfish," she stated bitterly. Then she fell quiet, feeling even shakier than she had before.

"I'm sorry," he muttered. "I didn't know."

"No, you didn't know, but you didn't want to know either."

"That's not the first time you've mentioned that," he pointed out, his voice steady.

She looked over at him. "No, it's not, and it probably won't be the last," she admitted, with a shrug. "You always acted as if everything was perfect in your world, and yet it was nowhere near perfect. However, no way anybody who does energy work—as you do—couldn't have seen or felt how wrong it all was, ... unless you were deliberately blocking it. Unless you were intentionally shutting out everything, there is no reason you shouldn't have known that something was terribly wrong. I just think that, deep down, you didn't want to face what she was doing, so you made sure you didn't have to."

It was a proverbial slap in the face, and he took it. He sat in the driver's seat, … silent.

Angela sighed. "I get it, and maybe I also blocked it out for a long time too. Maybe I just couldn't handle seeing what she had done to me and to my relationship without blocking it out either," she murmured. "My sister left a destructive path in her wake, and then she skipped out in death and didn't have to face the music."

"That's hardly fair," he protested.

"Of course it's not fair," she snapped, then groaned. "Yet I'm still supposed to be fair, aren't I? I mean, she's dead. I can't speak ill of the dead. I can't tell the truth or say anything that would make people think badly of her because, after all, she's dead, murdered even. *Poor Sadie*," she quipped, and then she groaned.

"And that makes me sound like a cold-hearted bitch, and I'm sorry for that," she acknowledged, "but there is a limit to how much I'm willing to hide. I kept so much about her to myself for so long because you just weren't ready to hear it. And now that it's been unleashed, that bitterness will tumble around for a while, until I can get a handle on it again," she noted, hating the fact that she couldn't control it.

"However, what I can tell you is this. … I knew she would lie. I knew that she would cheat and that she would have other relationships. She told me that my fiancé—the man I had loved with all my heart—wasn't good enough for me and that I needed to see the truth of the matter. When I replied that she wasn't good enough for him, she laughed and admitted that neither of them was very good, and she sure as hell wouldn't be taking a step down from you.

"When I asked her how she could even do that to you, she just laughed and said, *Riff doesn't give a crap*. That offended me at the time, but maybe she was right. You didn't see what you didn't want to see, and she kept it that way. Of course she used energy work against you too," she added, shaking her head. "That was her little game. She liked to think that she was pulling one over on you, that you didn't know. Yet she didn't seem to think that you finding out would be a problem either."

Riff appeared stunned into silence and just stared out the windshield, as Angela kept talking.

"Somewhere along the line, either she thought you would be totally okay with it or you would never find out. Even if you did, you wouldn't care. I don't know how that happened in her world or in yours," she noted, "but, damn, ... she certainly had you fooled."

"And you're angry with me?" he asked, his tone flat, chilled.

"Yeah, I am. If you had seen it beforehand, you might have been able to let her go and to not be so persistent about all this. Do I want answers? Hell yes, I want answers, but it's not fair that I should feel guilty about keeping all this ugliness from you," she snapped. "You're making me feel even more guilt, and I don't like it." With that, she turned, pulled her knees up, and leaned against the passenger side door, closing her eyes.

"You'll really sleep after that?" he asked, almost mocking her.

She didn't say anything because the last thing she wanted was to deal with more of this BS. She was ripped apart inside, everything opened and exposed, the scars built up over the last many years ripped off, the wounds bleeding again, a slow welling of blood that she didn't even know how to stop, didn't even know if stopping was possible.

She'd been to hell and back over all this. The guilt ripped into her, for hating her sister, for knowing that Sadie didn't deserve murder, even if she did deserve to pay for her crimes. But then why was Angela just blaming Sadie? Angela's own ex had been in the middle of it too.

"One of the hardest things was when she was murdered, and my ex-fiancé was a wreck over it. He went to pieces because she wasn't there anymore." Angela gave a bitter laugh. "It had literally just been a matter of a few days since I'd found out about them," she noted. "He and I were over, completely over. Not that he was necessarily even looking to continue with me once he got involved with my sister and *fell in love*, according to him. Even though she was just playing a game, there was nobody else for him, so she destroyed his life too."

"And yours," he said.

"Yeah, but nobody ever gave a shit about mine," she murmured, hating that well of bitterness still inside her. "Listen to me. I'm still struggling with what she did to my world years ago."

"I'm sure she had a lot to say at the end, didn't she?"

"Oh, you have no idea," she murmured. "Nothing good and definitely nothing fair and some of it was pretty rough to take."

"She got like that when she was angry," Riff said.

"You mean, when she felt she had been robbed of something she wanted or when she failed to get something she thought she should have, but somebody else got it instead? She was like a two-year-old in a sandbox and took her most brutal revenge at all times."

"Yeah, she was like that," he agreed sadly. "She was so very full of life and so very full of poison at times."

"Yeah? She had all you guys wrapped around her fingers," she murmured. "You've been pining away for her for a very long time, and, now that you find out the truth, you're still denying it and won't see her for who she really was."

"Can you blame me?" he asked in a calm tone. Almost too calm. "If you hadn't come across them in bed that day, a truth that you could no longer ignore, you would be sitting here right beside me, crying out against the evidence we just saw."

"And yet we don't even know that it was evidence of Sadie's murder yet," she pointed out.

"You're right," Riff replied. "We have to wait for the DNA to come back."

"How long will that take?"

"Normally it could take six weeks or more, but Jonas put a rush on it. With any luck we'll find out tomorrow or the next day. We've worked a few cases for him lately, and this last one got dicey, so that may be why he's going the extra mile here."

"If we're lucky, we'll find out tomorrow, and the conjecture can stop."

"Maybe, but all that does is open up a lot more questions."

"Not in my mind. Never again. Sadie met somebody *again*, had an affair *again*, played around *again*. Only this time, she picked somebody really slimy and got herself killed."

"Yet James mentioned talk about it being because of somebody around Sadie."

"And who would that have been? Me, you, my fiancé, the Chip guy that James mentioned, the latest guy she was sleeping with at the time, or someone else? For a case with no suspects, this just opens up the pool to way-too-many more, and who the hell needs that shit?"

He shrugged and nodded. "I still want to find the answers."

"I'm glad you still do, even after learning about all this," she muttered, slouching against the door again, "but I'm done for the moment. My mind is exhausted, and I don't like very much about today, so I'll just curl up in the back." With that, she climbed over the front seat and settled into the back seat.

"So much for your driving."

"You would never let me anyway. Wake me up when we get close to home."

With that, she closed her eyes and resolutely tried to fall asleep.

THEY WERE ALMOST at the castle when Riff reached back and gave her a rough shake. He kept his gaze on the road.

Angela opened her eyes and studied him with an odd look.

"What's wrong?" he asked, staring at her.

She shrugged. "It doesn't matter." She sat up and looked around. "We're almost home. Good. I'm exhausted."

"Yeah, and you got to sleep most of the way," he noted humorously.

She shrugged. "Yeah, I did, but you could have asked me to drive at any time."

"I'm fine," he said, shaking his head.

Angela snorted. "I know you're fine. You're always fine, and that's the motto, isn't it? *Everything's good. You're okay,* and, if you keep believing it, then you won't have to face the reality that something other than perfection is in your world."

He sighed. "Look. I get that, for you, I did the worst thing possible, but I guess maybe I was just in survival mode myself."

She hesitated, shifting her position, then climbing back into the front seat before she looked over at him. "So, do you believe it? Do you believe me?"

"I believe you. I have no reason to think you would lie to me at this point. As for the mattress, I want proof, something more, the DNA," he stated.

"Yeah, I get that. As for me, no, I don't have any reason to lie to you," she added. "I know you probably blame me for not telling you before, but considering the timing—"

"I know," he interrupted, "considering the timing and the fight between the two of you, it makes sense. Ironically, at the time, I was trying to get her to talk to you and to make up, so everything would be fine, but now I can see why that wouldn't ever work."

"Yeah, *ya* think?" she asked, with a snort. "My sister could be brutal, but, for the most part, she kept that brutality for other people, not me."

"*Huh,* doesn't seem like it right now. Any idea why or what set her off on this pathway? I've spent most of this drive wondering if I just did too many missions and just wasn't there enough or what."

"Babies," Angela declared. He looked at her, startled. She shrugged. "Sadie wanted babies."

"I never said no," he snapped, clenching the steering wheel.

"Yet we found out that Sadie couldn't have any."

He swore at that. "God damn it. Secrets and lies all round. Was anybody ever gonna tell me that?"

"No, probably not. I think maybe she thought the main sire was causing the problem, how her affairs might fix the issue."

He gave a snort at that. "So, she thought I was shooting blanks, but, rather than find out for sure, she checks it out by having sex with a lot of other men to see if she can get pregnant? Then what? Pass the baby off as mine?"

"Yeah, probably. I wouldn't put it past her."

"So, that's how you found out you can't have kids either, isn't it?"

"It's how I found out that there's a good chance I can't have any myself," she corrected. "I haven't gone through the same process and tests, but one of the times that she came to me, she shared that she didn't think she could and told me what she'd learned so far. At my suggestion, she did go to a couple specialists, who confirmed that she couldn't have children and that it's hereditary. So it's possible, maybe even likely, that I could be in the same position," she explained. "I don't know. I haven't confronted that yet. Sadie went off the rails at that point."

"So, more guilt on your part."

"Yes, more guilt to deal with, yes," she confirmed. "However, it was also about my future too, and I didn't even get the chance to deal with that because she died soon afterward."

"So, by then, she figured she couldn't get pregnant any-way at that point, so she might as well just play around because there would be no repercussions?"

"I don't know, but that's possible and maybe was part of it." Angela shrugged. "Look. Sadie was my sister, but she was also your fiancée, so why don't you start answering some of these questions for yourself?"

"I would if I could," he shared, "but I've been sitting here this whole drive home trying to figure out what I missed so completely and how I could have missed it."

"As far as I'm concerned, you just didn't want to see it. That and Sadie using her energy skills on you. That's the only way you could have missed it."

"You know saying that on repeat will just make me an-grier."

"As if I care," she snapped. He looked at her, startled, and she shrugged. "I get it. It's all shitty news, and it's coming at you all at once right now. You didn't expect it, but I still have to deal with it, and so do you. It's just the situation we're in. Yeah, I knew she was screwing around on you, but, since she was screwing around with my fiancé, my world was suddenly upside down, and I didn't feel like updating you about it. *My bad, so sorry.* But right now, we do have a chance to open this up and to find out who killed her. So, I, for one, want that resolved. Then I can get on with my life and won't feel so angry and bitter and guilty all the damn time."

"Oh, I get it," Riff muttered. "I'm still in the angry part."

"Sorry, but you're not even there yet," she snapped yet again, as she glared at him. "Wait until you get DNA confirmation. Then, when you least expect it, you'll be hit by a ton of bricks. You won't know what you did wrong and why you weren't enough, why she wouldn't have told you, why, why, why, why. There will be no answers because she's not here to answer anything."

He felt his own temper rising again. "Which is another reason why it would have been nice if you had said something to me at the time."

"Yeah, if only I knew that Sadie would die soon, that would have been great, wouldn't it?" She laughed. "My sister already had you wrapped around her little finger, so all she would have done was lie and would make you hate me too." He frowned at her. She shrugged. "She would have told you that I was making a big to-do about nothing, that it wasn't true, and how in the hell could you possibly ever believe such a thing? How she would *never* be unfaithful. She loved you, *blah, blah, blah*," she offered, with a wave of her hand.

"You would have believed Sadie just like you always believed her—because you wanted to believe her. The fact of the matter is, it wouldn't have done either one of us any good to have told you, so whatever." She shifted again in her seat. "Jesus, I know I needed to come today, but, damn, I really just want to go away for a holiday and not face anybody right now."

"They will all know when we walk in there."

"They will all know something, and they will all want details," she agreed. "We can't keep it under wraps and expect them to help us. Are you ready for that?"

He stiffened. "Ready? No."

Angela sighed. "Will they be accepting and neutral about it?"

"Hopefully. Otherwise, if they get in my face, I'll push back," Riff warned. "Yet they're people like us," he reminded her, glancing her way. "They read energies too and do want what's best for us, and that's the part that makes it hard to walk away from Terk and his people."

"I know," she muttered. "I find I keep coming back."

"Are you sure it's not because of the babies?" he asked.

"No, I'm not sure it's *not* the babies," she replied, glaring at him. "It all depends on how my own biology is working. I don't have a clue."

"You might want to ask Cara and Clary if they can do something about it." When Angela frowned at him, he sighed. "You've helped them a lot, I understand, coming at odd hours and not charging them anywhere close to what you could have. So maybe you should be asking for a little help for yourself. We've got some incredible healers."

"I've heard that," she conceded reluctantly. "Maybe in the back of my mind I always wondered. I also don't know that I *do* have a problem."

"That doesn't mean there isn't something Clary and Cara could do," he noted. "The stuff they do is freaking amazing."

"I don't really talk to them about what they do," she admitted, "outside of the massive number of babies in the place."

"I think they've got that under control now."

"*Ya* think? I would guess that had to be a priority."

He grinned. "I'm pretty sure it was a priority, at least until people choose to have more," he noted. "But really, if you do have a health problem, I gotta tell you. That's the one place to get pregnant."

She laughed. "Then it would almost be worth it."

"Almost worth what?"

"Bringing a partner into their place for the night, just to

get pregnant," she muttered. "Because, hell yeah, I want babies. I want a family. I always have, and it will be a hardship if I can't have them, but I sure as hell won't go on a humpy-dumpy spree just to make myself feel better," she muttered.

He winced. "Do you really have to use that term?"

"Probably not," she admitted, "but it feels appropriate."

Riff couldn't say anything to that, so he snapped his mouth closed. After a moment, he suggested, "Please don't use it in front of this crowd."

She groaned. "That's the thing. Everything I say about my sister comes back to haunt me."

"No, it's not that," he muttered. "It's an issue when everything you say about your sister is also about my fiancée, and I'm not fully adjusted to anything that we just found out today."

"And they'll know that too."

He groaned. "So, I'll have a lot of gazes on me."

"Yeah, you will," she stated. "So remember that part about how good it is to be a member of a large family?"

"And yet I'm still a loner," he added.

"Oh, trust me. I've noticed," she said smoothly. "I've also noticed how quickly you run every time I'm in the vicinity, as if I have the plague or something."

"I do not," he declared in shock.

She burst out laughing. "The hell you don't," she spat. "I can't believe you're still lying to yourself." She shook her head. "You need to get out of that habit and fast."

"Gee, thanks," he murmured, as he pulled up in front of the castle. He stopped, turned off the engine, and announced, "We're home."

Such a fatalistic tone filled his words that Angela stared

out the passenger window at the front door and sighed. "Yeah, and now comes the hard part."

"For you and me both," he muttered.

"It's harder in some ways for you," she noted, "because this is the first time you're hearing it, and, for that, I truly am sorry."

"Stop saying you're sorry, damn it," he snapped. "I'm not somebody who has to be hugged and held over bad news. The good news is that it was a long time ago. The bad news is, I still don't understand it. When I can understand it, then maybe. … But what you shared about pregnancy does give me some insight into why with Sadie."

"And I guess the why matters, doesn't it?"

He looked at her and nodded carefully. "The why always matters, whether the guy stole the bread to feed his family or he's a klepto off his meds," he declared. "In fact, it's often everything. Without that motivation, there's really no understanding why somebody did something, and, in this case, I really need to know."

"Good luck with that," she muttered, adding an eye roll. "For all I know, she did it just because she could."

With that, Angela got out of the vehicle and slammed the door in his face.

CHAPTER 5

ANGELA WALKED INTO the castle, feeling the wonderful homecoming atmosphere and the air of expectancy within.

It felt like home.

Sometimes home, sometimes not, always full of interesting events, characters, and people. And, of course, whether that was good or bad, it was a place she associated with Riff.

Ignoring the three men, who were all heading toward the dining room area where Terkel waited, Angela just went straight up to her bedroom. As she got up to the second floor, where her room was down on the far side, a nearby door opened, and Clary called out. Angela hesitated and asked, "Did you need me?" She hoped against hope that all was well.

Clary smiled at her. "No, but I think you need me."

Her eyebrows shot up. "I just need to go to bed and to have some time to assimilate."

"Yes, you need that too," Clary agreed, as she pulled her inside her suite and pointed to a chair in front of her. "Sit." Angela hesitated, and Clary just stared at her. Finally Angela sat down. "I'm fine, you know?"

"Yeah, sure you are," Clary murmured. "You've had some rough days. Today could have gone in many different directions, but it feels very much like it was a hard day."

"You don't need to be tapping into my psyche," Angela said. "You guys have enough here to deal with."

"We do, but, even though you don't seem to realize it, you are part of this place, of these people," Clary shared, "and, when something happens to you, we recognize it."

"Well, damn," she muttered. "In that case, this next little while could get rough."

"We know that," Clary noted, as she placed her hands on Angela's shoulders. "What you don't realize or haven't been able to acknowledge yet is that you're not alone."

"That's because it feels as if I'm always alone," she murmured. "You guys have been great at making me feel welcome and all, but there is no doubt that inside, with all the rest of this going on, I do feel alone. So, until this is settled, that's probably just the way it'll be. Hopefully, after that, I can move on."

"And, in the meantime, your emotions will be everywhere, and you could use a little bit of healing yourself."

Angela twisted and looked at her. "Is that what this is about?"

"Sure," Clary confirmed.

The healer gently soothed Angela's shoulders, Clary's fingers squeezing, not quite massaging, almost as if testing a dough to see if it was ready. Even that analogy made Angela laugh. "You don't have to, you know?"

"Of course, I don't have to," Clary agreed, with a smile. "That makes it even more important that I do so. We recognize that this is a tough time for you, and we also recognize that quite possibly it'll get a lot uglier, and, for you, it will be an unsettling time."

"Unsettling," she repeated, moving the word around in her mouth as if tasting it. "I don't know if that's the word I would use, but you're right. It's definitely not an easy time."

"Tell me what you found out today," Clary suggested. Angela gave her a brief version of the day's events. When she got to the motel part and their wait now for the forensic results to see if it really was her sister, Clary murmured, "You believe it was her, don't you?"

"Don't you?"

"I do," she agreed.

"Wait a minute, you weren't surprised about the affair." She hesitated, but Clary's hands continued to soothe her shoulders, both hands moving as if pulling invisible weights or troubles away from her.

"Of course you had personal reasons too," Clary added, with a heavy sigh.

"Yes, I did," Angela replied, her voice catching in the back of her throat.

Knowing that Clary was seeing something and probably would keep prodding until Angela came clean, she told her about her sister and her fiancé. Clary didn't say anything, and, for that, Angela was grateful.

There never seemed to be any judgment with these women, just an acceptance that people were people, and they came with the good and the bad and the ugly. No matter what you did, there was only so much anybody could ever do to deal with betrayal.

When Angela finally ran down, Clary worked on the top of her head, as if opening old wounds and pulling out old energy, painful energy. For Angela, it was just a moment to relax and to forget about the pain, to forget about all she'd gone through, but the guilt? The guilt remained. The guilt was still the hardest. "How does one ever deal with guilt?" she murmured.

Clary began, "I can tell you until I'm blue in the face that it's a useless emotion, that those you feel guilty about don't give a crap and that everything you're feeling can be validated in many other ways without destroying your body." Clary sighed. "Yet every time I've spoken to anybody about guilt, there really hasn't been any way to ease it for them. It's something you must let go of yourself."

"How do you do that?" Angela asked. "I feel so guilty that my sister is gone. Yet at the same time I feel guilty because a part of me is happy about it." She was too bitter, and her voice cracked.

"And is that because of Riff?"

She hesitated, unsure of what to say, and then just gave in. "Of course you can see that too, can't you?"

"Yes," Clary noted, "and it really does help alleviate a lot of the confusion for us bystanders."

"Maybe," Angela muttered, "but it also opens up that feeling of being raw and open to criticism and just so vulnerable," she murmured.

"And that very vulnerability allows me to do as much healing as I can get done right now," Clary shared. "So, I understand that sense of invasion that you're quite possibly feeling, but you also need to know that what you're feeling is totally normal and that what your sister did to you was wrong. Not to mention, I don't in any way know and understand all she did to you."

Angela stilled. "Do I want to know what you're saying?"

"Not necessarily, but I do feel she affected your energy more than you suspect. I think it was sisterly rivalry or outright jealousy, although the source of that I can't see. I think you need to spend some time looking at the relationship you had with her and see in what way she could have used her energy against you. Anything done to harm is wrong."

"I don't think she thought it was wrong," Angela pointed out. "I don't think she thought about it at all. I think, if she wanted something, she took it."

"Was it to teach you a lesson?"

"I think it was to get back at me."

"Interesting, but get back at you how? Why?"

"I think she was afraid that I could have children, something she never could have. Yet I don't know whether I can or can't. I am still figuring that out. I've held off doing any testing because the results were so traumatic for Sadie. I'm trying to get to a place where I don't care, and then maybe I'll go through with the testing—or maybe not."

"A dangerous place when you don't care, and that's a very hard thing to achieve. Particularly if any part of you ever wanted a family."

"That doesn't mean I want to have a family necessarily," she clarified. "I mean, it's the field I went into, and it only makes sense that I went into it because I love babies."

"It also makes sense that you might have gone into it because you were afraid you couldn't have children."

"I don't know that I'm afraid that I can or I can't. I went into this field before this question ever came up," she pointed out. "A couple women on my side of the family couldn't conceive, but it's not something I had discussed with any of them. They were all generations older, and I don't have any connection with them."

Clary didn't say anything, just kept working on Angela's system.

Slowly Angela felt some of that tight coil inside her was unwinding, relaxing. Underlying it all was a sensation of coming undone, so instead Angela focused her inner eye on coils that had been wound too tight, now relaxing the coils had them in a more natural position. "I don't know what you're doing, but it feels wonderful," she shared impulsively.

"Good."

At Clary's urgings, Angela took several deep breaths, feeling more unwinding within. When she sat back and slowly stretched out her arms, leaning forward and stretching her back, Clary smiled at her and said, "That should feel better."

"It feels great," she admitted. "If that's something you do on a regular basis, you're truly blessed."

"I do this on a regular basis, but I do this and many other forms of healing," she added. "However, for somebody like your sister, this form of healing probably wasn't available to her."

"That was another problem between us. She had abilities, but she didn't see that they had any value, and she didn't necessarily utilize them in any way that made sense."

"Oh, she utilized them," Clary countered, with a wry smile. "Maybe more to entice rather than to do good."

Angela stiffened at that. "Jesus, I didn't even think of that."

"That's because you were so full of anger that you couldn't see past it."

Angela sucked in her breath, twisting to look up at her. "Do you think that's why my fiancé did what he did?"

"I think it's quite possible," Clary replied.

"Does that make him less culpable?" Angela asked.

"In some ways, yes."

"Does it let him off the hook?" Angela added.

"No, because, at the end of the day, he wouldn't have

done it if he hadn't wanted to."

She nodded. "Right, and it all comes back to that ability of hers to twist and to turn things in the most disturbing ways, leaving others to deal with the mess she left behind. Even this time."

Clary nodded. "Murder is messy. Murder leaves unanswered questions. Murder leaves people grieving and wondering why. In this case, you have no idea why she was in that motel room or what series of events took her there. I'm sure Riff is dealing with a lot of those same questions himself."

"Absolutely," she agreed, her tone heavy. "You can bet I'm not the best person to help him through it. He blames me for not having told him." Clary frowned at her in surprise. Angela nodded. "He seems to think I was supposed to tell him that his fiancée had an affair with my fiancé, and maybe I should have. I don't know. It wasn't in me at the time, and I was still dealing with my own shock and sense of betrayal at the hands of my own damn sister," she admitted.

"I understand it wasn't long afterward that she was killed, so would that have been the time to bring it up?"

"Maybe, but I still couldn't have done it. Riff was already grieving, and I knew he wouldn't understand, and he certainly wouldn't thank the messenger," she stated in a dry tone.

Clary smiled. "And that would have hurt you even more."

Angela winced. "I know you can see that I love the man. And that I have probably loved him since time began, but he was my sister's and could never be mine, so I moved on. Still, it really doesn't help me to know that so many other people recognize what's going on in my heart. These are private feelings that I haven't shared with him."

Clary gave her the gentlest smile, almost piercing right through her. "You may not see the value, but it does help other people to understand how and why. Nothing is easy about love. Nothing is easy about any of this," she murmured. "We healers aren't here to judge. We aren't here to even look at all the lines of script in someone's life to see how people act or feel, to see what they've done or not done in their lives," she explained.

Clary continued. "We're trying to find a way to help people through that and in whatever form that comes. And it's usually not the form we ever think that it'll be." She patted Angela on the shoulder. "The fact that you are connected to Riff... is something that Riff must come to terms with. It's not something you can do. I understand that, in many ways, your relationship with your fiancé was possible because you thought that Riff was unattainable."

"He *was* unattainable. He was my sister's partner," she declared, staring at Clary. "That took him off the table. For me at least. That's a line I would never cross."

"Which is also why you're so angry at your sister because she didn't live by your rules. What was off the table for you was not off the table for her."

Angela winced at that and then slowly nodded. "If you want to look at it that way, that's very true. I didn't really realize how hurt Sadie might have been over the baby thing either. I hadn't really considered it before. Still, that's no excuse. She didn't need to do this to me, but her point was that I was better off to know that my choice in partner was so lousy that she could turn his attention without any effort. Of course it was also a diss against me because, as far as she was concerned, I couldn't hold a man."

"And if you try to remember that your sister was hurting, literally hurting to the point that she couldn't contemplate anything else in her life, and felt her only move was to strike out, hurting those closest to her, it might make it a lot easier for you."

"I thought …" Angela began. "I thought I had dealt with so much of this already. I even sought help. And now? … Well, it's all coming back up again."

"Yeah, life has a way of doing that," Clary noted. "At least you should be able to get some sleep now."

"I am tired, that's for sure," Angela acknowledged, as she slowly got up, almost stumbling as the blood rushed to her head. "I hope I can sleep. That would be a huge gift tonight."

Clary smiled. "Now go. Get some rest." Clary opened the door for her and nudged her toward her apartment.

Weaving back and forth, feeling exhausted beyond the ability to function, Angela stumbled toward her suite and straight to bed.

RIFF THREW HIMSELF down into the big chair in front of the fire. The others had gone to bed, so now it was just him and Terkel, who handed him a scotch on the rocks. Riff considered it, smiled, and added, "I'm really not much of a drinker."

Terkel nodded. "Neither am I, but, every once in a while, … we all need a little something."

"Yeah," Riff grumbled, as he picked up the glass and took a sip. "Every once in a while, it does seem to be just the right thing to do."

"Particularly now, when you're grieving all over again."

"Maybe," he conceded, "but, if this is grieving, why is there no grief?"

"Do you want to talk about it?" Terkel asked, his tone quiet, the timbre of his voice mellow as it resonated through the room. Firelight danced on the furniture around them, and no other light was on in the space.

Immediately Riff shook his head, but his mind seemed to have won an argument with his mouth because almost immediately the words skipped out of him. "She was in a motel with another man, and it sounds like it wasn't anything close to the first time." Riff's tone was harsh, filled with anger and stiff with pain. "How the hell do you reconcile that?"

Terkel didn't say anything for a long moment, as if waiting to see if anything else would come out, but Riff had already shared more than he had intended to and even now felt foolish. "Forget it. I mean, it's my problem, not yours."

"It's everybody's problem when it's something like this," Terk replied. "I do have a question though. Was there any indication that your relationship was in trouble?"

Riff snorted. "I wouldn't be quite so stunned at hearing this news if there had been," he said in anguish. "I was gone a lot, and she told me that she was fine with my absences, but apparently she wasn't fine with it at all. To find out this way is even worse, and apparently, to top it all off, Angela knew. She knew all of it, in part because Sadie was having an affair with Angela's fiancé, of all people." Terkel just sat here. "I know I shouldn't blame Angela, and I can't believe Sadie would have done that to her own sister."

"What was the relationship between the two of them like?"

Riff grimaced and then admitted, "Not great. There were definitely issues between them, but I wouldn't have thought that was something Sadie would ever do. I don't think Angela thought it was something her sister would do either, which is why I'm sure, from Angela's perspective, her sense of betrayal was rough as well. Of course I had nothing good to say about it, and I was angrier than anything because she didn't tell me."

"Would you have believed her earlier?"

He gave a harsh laugh as he lifted the scotch glass and had a long sip. "Probably not," he conceded. "No, I wouldn't have, not a chance."

"Why not?"

"I was pretty sure that my relationship was strong and in solid shape," he stated bitterly. "Even now I'm sitting here, wondering what I missed. Maybe—as Angela said—it had everything to do with Sadie not being able to have children."

"What do you think?" Terk asked.

"I don't know what I think. Sadie never asked me to be tested or even asked, if she couldn't have children, would that be an issue for me. She never once brought it up. If she had, I would have been more than happy to see what our options were. Whether I needed something or she needed something, whatever, I would have done anything she asked." He shook his head. "It wasn't ever discussed, so I didn't even know it was an issue. So, what kind of a fiancé was I if I didn't even know it was an issue?"

"A man whose fiancée couldn't talk about it," Terkel stated. "I get that, for a while, the guilt is likely to be pretty crippling."

Riff stared at Terkel. "It has been crippling because I couldn't solve her murder. I mean, that's what I supposedly do for a living, and here I haven't had anything to tell her."

"Angela?" Terk asked, confused, reminding Riff that he was skipping through the explanations and going from topic to topic, going from Sadie to Angela.

"Yeah, I didn't have anything to tell Angela. It's why I've half avoided her all this time. I didn't have answers, and yet I should have. I should have had something, and now I'm sitting here, half out of my mind, with no clue where to start, because now I'm wondering if I even knew my fiancée. And, if I did, how well?"

"I gathered as much." Terkel brought him a refill.

"How is this even … I want to say, *How is it fair*, which is stupid. Of course it's not fair. It's not fair at all, but I don't even know what to do with this new information," he admitted. "It all feels so wrong."

"That's another question to ask yourself, I guess. Could it be wrong? Could Sadie's reason for being there have been something completely different?"

Riff stared at him as he swirled the glass in his hand. "As much as I want to believe that there could be another explanation, I'm afraid that this explanation is correct," he conceded. "Yet my need to not have been taken in is asking me to find another reason for all this. Nobody wants to be the dupe in this, and apparently that's exactly what I was."

Terkel let him vent.

"Then there's Angela," Riff whispered. "I owe her an apology. … I really hate it when I screw up like that."

Terkel, his voice gentle now, added, "I don't think anybody considers it a screw up when you initially find out that somebody who you loved for a very long time wasn't quite the person you thought she was. So, cut yourself some slack, and go easy on yourself. I don't think Angela's expecting anything from you."

"No, … she's not," he confirmed. "I made it pretty clear that I was plenty pissed off at her."

"And you can fix that in the morning," Terkel announced, getting up. "What we need is confirmation on the DNA, and that will give us a way to go forward."

"You might need confirmation, and I did tell Angela that I needed confirmation, but I see energy, remember? Even old forgotten and faded energy from years ago."

"What did you see?" Terk asked.

"I could see my fiancée's energy all over that damn bed, and it wasn't a *sit back and relax, have a cup of coffee* kind of energy. She was an active participant in whatever the hell went on, until it went very ugly for whatever reason," he shared. "If I could have read the crime scene back then, I might have been able to see everything." He shuddered, as if to get rid of that mental image.

"If I'd known she was having an affair, it might have sent me in this direction," he acknowledged, the fury once again building. "But never in a million years would I have put her in a sleazy motel at the edge of town with a criminal," he muttered. "Not in a million years."

At that, he tossed back the rest of his scotch, looked over at Terkel, and added, "I'm going to bed."

CHAPTER 6

ANGELA WOKE UP early, feeling wonderful. She shifted in bed, exclaiming as she got up, wondering at how free from the expected stiffness and pain her body was. She had expected to be achy, tired, and worn out, but whatever Clary had done had performed miracles, and Angela owed her a huge debt of gratitude for it.

She hadn't considered just how much these twin energy-working healers could do, and, now having experienced the tiniest bit, Angela was excited to learn more about how talented, how gifted these two women were. In truth Angela was envious with all that these energy workers could do.

That just brought up more memories of her sister, who had much stronger skills than Angela had. Sadie had laughed at her about it. When they were young, it had seemed as if Angela had been equally gifted. However, around puberty, her sister's abilities had flourished, while Angela's appeared to have died altogether. Even then the two hadn't really known what to do with this skill. For herself, it was instinctive to go into the healing arts. Angela had long tried to persuade her sister to follow suit, but her sister was all about a good time, not a working time.

And to see what the healers living with Terk could do? … Well …

Angela herself did have some healing energy she could

pull on, but, wow, nothing like this. Of course, that voice in the back of her mind always nudged her, making her wonder what could be. If the healers could take what she had already, maybe they could teach her how to do some of this healing work, and maybe Angela could have a bigger impact on her patients.

Pondering that, she dressed and headed to the kitchen. There she found Clary, sitting at the dining table. Angela walked over, gave her hug, and whispered, "Thank you. I feel wonderful."

Clary looked up and smiled. "Good. You really needed to unwind last night."

"I didn't even know I did," she admitted with a smile, as she walked over to the coffeepot, poured herself a cup, and sat down. "Where is everybody?"

"With the kids," she replied, with a chuckle. "It's nine."

Angela stared at her in shock and checked her phone. "Oh my God, I really slept in, didn't I?"

"You did," Terkel confirmed, as he walked in, and right behind him was Riff.

She stiffened slightly and then relaxed. "Did you get any sleep?" she asked Riff, refusing to back away from him and whatever unpleasantness he might want to dish out this morning.

He shrugged. "Not as good as you, from the looks of it," he noted, eyeing her quizzically. "You seem to have gotten some actual rest—and a lot of it."

"I did. I wouldn't have, but Clary did some wonderful healing work before I went to bed last night," she murmured. "So, from that perspective, I'm feeling pretty great."

"Ah, good for you," Riff replied, without adding anything else to the conversation. He walked over and poured himself some coffee, before sitting down beside her.

"Have we had any news?" she asked into the silence.

He shook his head. "None that I know of so far." He looked over at Terkel, who just shook his head.

Terk shrugged. "I haven't heard anything yet, but I'm expecting it at any time."

She nodded. "I think we're all waiting for the phone to ring, and that sense of doom will crash down on us when we find out for sure."

At that, Riff stared at her. "You aren't sure?"

"Oh no, I am sure, but nothing like having that certainty validated by science," she murmured.

"I agree with you there," he said. "Still, just because the science might be there, it still won't necessarily give us the answers we're looking for."

"Sometimes there just aren't any answers," she grumbled, staring at him defiantly. "She's gone, and there isn't anything we can do to change that."

When the sound of a phone ringing in the distance broke the silence, Angela looked around to see who it was. When no one came into the dining room, she sat here, just wondering.

A few minutes later, Celia entered the doorway, looking over at them, and nodded. "Okay, time for a powwow."

"In what way?" Riff asked warily.

"That was the lab, confirming that it was, indeed, Sadie, and … they picked up two other DNAs. One they matched to someone who had been in the prison system, a Johnny Waco. As for the other one, we don't have any answers as to who that is. He might have survived his injuries."

"He's not in the prison system?"

"Not governmental," she replied. "Afraid not, and he's

not come up in any of our databases either. We're running it through Interpol now. Yet he could be some petty thief who just spent days in a jail cell here and there, which isn't included in these bigger databases."

Riff sat so quiet and so still at her side that Angela was afraid he would shatter at any moment. She wanted to protect him, but there was no protection from this ugliness. "So, now that we know," she spoke, her voice barely audible, "what does that tell us?"

"It tells us that the primary crime scene is a completely different story now," Terkel replied. "We need to find out who that third party was and who else could have been in that room that night. And who else might have been in the vicinity, either connected to our threesome in the motel room or maybe just witnesses. We need to start from scratch again."

She nodded slowly. "And yet starting from scratch isn't the easiest because it's been five years now."

"Exactly," Terk confirmed. "So we'll reopen the case from start to finish, and so will MI5."

"MI5," she repeated. "That's not the right department, is it?"

"Not what you would expect, but apparently Johnny Waco was involved with a group of homegrown terrorists."

"Seriously?" she asked. She turned to Riff. "James mentioned the mob, so this seems to be another confirmation." Riff didn't reply.

Terk nodded. "It was kept hush hush, but now that Waco's murder is being reopened, MI5 must be on the periphery."

"Fine," she muttered. "But the less government interference, the better, right?"

"Oh, absolutely," Terk agreed, sending a smile in her direction. "Yet we'll need everybody's help. Otherwise we won't get anywhere."

"I'm not arguing with you on that point," she clarified, settling back and hugging the cup of coffee in front of her. "I was just hoping that, if we had something, we could get somewhere. Yet starting over again isn't easy."

"Meaning?" Terkel asked her quizzically.

"Going back and interviewing people again isn't really an option because memories have changed, details are a blur, five years have passed, and nobody ..." She looked over at Riff, then quickly changed what she would say. "I would add that nobody gives a shit," she clarified, flushing at her words, "and, of course, that's not quite right."

"But it's close enough," Riff agreed from her side, "because you're right. Nobody gives a shit. It's been just long enough that everybody is to the point of thinking, *Just put it behind you and move on*," he declared, staring at her.

She winced. "That comment was directed at me of course."

"I don't know that it's directed at you as much as it's just a fact of life," he stated, flint in his gaze. "When dealing with people in this criminal element, nobody cares. It's not about them, so we're just supposed to move on." He got up, walked over to the coffeepot, and refilled his cup, sitting back down again. "I'll be taking off for a few days," he announced to all, a finality in his tone. "I'll start at the beginning and see what I can do."

Such fatigue filled his tone that everyone glanced at each other. Terkel zeroed in on Riff and stated, "Working alone is not the smartest way to do it. We do have a lot of people here, and we can help. ... Prolonging this will just make the pain that much worse."

Riff stared at him. He frowned at his cup of coffee, obviously not sure what to say or to do.

Langdon appeared, along with Royce. Langdon interjected, "I'm in. Whoever the hell this murderer is has gotten away with it for way too long. It's time for some closure and some justice," he stated. "I know that feelings and emotions are pretty high and confused right now, as everybody is trying to figure out what sent this supposedly happily engaged woman to a motel with a criminal, but the answers are out there, and we need to find them."

Not mincing his words and yet keeping it upright and honest had the rest of them in the room reacting in the same way, and, for that, Angela was grateful. "I do know that my sister was unhappy about the fact that she couldn't have children. I'm pretty sure that's what sent her off the rails. However, what sent her into the arms of these two men at that motel, I couldn't say. She did start drinking heavily at that point, and, by the end, she was heavily hooked." Riff turned and frowned at her. Angela shrugged and nodded. "She kept it from you."

"Jesus," he muttered. "If we went out for dinner, ... she would never even have a glass of wine with me."

"Because she was probably afraid that, if she had a little bit, ... she would have too much," Angela murmured. "She was not good at stopping once she got started. I don't think she wanted you to know about that." He sat back, his face grim, and she realized how it sounded. "I think she was just really messed up at the end. She hadn't come to terms with her childless future. She hadn't come to terms with what, to her, was a major failure as a woman. ... She didn't know how to tell you."

He didn't say anything, just nodded.

Feeling as if she had gotten off the hook easily, Angela deliberately avoided getting into that discussion again and looked around at the men. "I don't even know where to begin," she admitted, "but I really want to help."

Terk suggested, "One way you can help is if you can talk to her friends, people you know, maybe bring up this new information and see if they had any idea of the friends this Johnny Waco hung out with."

"I can do that," she confirmed. "I still have contact with a few of them." She looked over at Riff. "Unless you want to do it."

He shook his head. "No, it's probably better if I'm not the one to do it," he replied, struggling to keep his tone flat. He pushed back his chair and got up. "I'll be back in a few minutes." And, with that, he turned and walked away.

As soon as he was gone, Angela looked over at Terkel. "Did I say something wrong?"

"No," he replied, reassuring her, "not at all."

Langdon added in a soft tone, "This is just one of those adjustments that he'll have to live with, and it won't be easy on him."

"No, of course not," she agreed, as she shook her head. "I can make excuses until I'm blue in the face, but it still doesn't change the fact that what my sister did was just plain shitty. Yet she didn't deserve to be murdered, so I'll start making phone calls." She got up from the dining table and looked back at the others, with a pleading expression. "Please keep me in the loop."

When they nodded, she headed up to her room to get the list of phone numbers she never expected to need again.

RIFF LOOKED UP from the paperwork he had in front of him, when he noticed that Terk approached. Riff had had the old original file reprinted and was looking it over, without really taking it all in. "So, we're back to the beginning, except there wasn't much to begin with." He motioned at the papers in front of him.

"Of course not," Terkel agreed, with a nod. "Her body was found on an overpass. She'd been stabbed multiple times. She was only partially dressed, and we all thought it was a random attack, kidnapping, sexual assault. Obviously everything we thought we knew back then was wrong, and now we need to refocus and to come up with a whole new theory."

"Oh, we know what the new theory is," Riff muttered, glaring at him. "She hung out with the wrong people, and somebody went after the guy she was with. She was at the wrong place at the wrong time."

"Yes, that fits nicely," Terkel noted, "but the simplest answers aren't necessarily the right answers. It's never that simple in our world."

"Does it need to be simple?" Riff asked curiously. "I mean, we know that she was at the motel. Her DNA has been confirmed. Good or bad, we also know that this Johnny Waco guy was there, and we know that semen was found as well. Presumably she was there for a tryst, and something went wrong."

"I can agree with that, in theory," Terkel replied.

"In theory?" Riff repeated, staring at Terk. "Do you think something else is going on?"

"No, I think that's probably correct. I don't just want to

get locked in on the affair part of it, when there's obvious potential for an awful lot more to be going on here," he clarified in an odd tone. "We're doing a full background on this Johnny Waco, but, so far, he appears to be some smuggler who had delusions of grandeur above his station. So, what we need to do now is get to all his known associates and go rattle some cages."

At that, Riff's expression changed to a feral grin. "Rattling cages would be good," he said softly. "I know I could really use the exercise."

Terkel rolled his eyes at him. "You and I both know you don't get to rattle much in the way of cages or anything else in this case," he pointed out. "No matter what your intent, it would come off too much like a revenge mission."

"It's not a revenge mission, but I definitely need to be in on the action," he declared, a warning in his tone. "So don't even think about pulling me off it."

Terkel shook his head. "No, I wouldn't do that," he stated, agreeing with him. "I get it. I understand what you're going through, and I'm hoping you'll be a little easier on Angela over it all."

"I'm hoping to be too," he muttered, looking away from him, "once I get past what feels like a betrayal from her too."

"Yet tell me, what was she supposed to do? No way you would have acknowledged that she could have been right five years ago, and no way you would have allowed her to walk away from sharing that information without making her pay for it."

He winced. "Am I that much of an asshole?"

"Sometimes, yeah, you are," Terkel confirmed cheerfully. "I know it, and you know it too."

He grumbled somewhat at that. "I wouldn't have

thought I was quite that bad."

"Of course not," Terk replied. "None of us ever want to consider ourselves that bad, but the bottom line is that something was always going on within this craziness, and trying to figure out *what* is our current challenge. I was hoping you would find something in this file to get started with."

"The only thing we can do is hope that Angela shakes something loose with her phone calls and that the deep background check on Johnny Waco comes up with something," Riff noted. "Otherwise the case has been sitting here cold for a very long time. We don't want it sitting there any longer."

Terkel nodded. "I'm with you there."

Angela walked in, wearing a frown on her face.

"I hope that frown is good news," Terk noted in a mild tone.

She turned to him and shrugged. "I guess it depends on what you mean by good news. First, finding out that a mutual friend knew about Sadie's relationship with my fiancé, well, that was a little disturbing," she began coolly. "But finding out that she also knew about Sadie's relationship with Johnny Waco too? … That was a little much."

"Who was this?" Riff asked.

"Tamara."

"I remember her." Riff frowned. "They were quite old friends, weren't they? Sadie used to go off and see her all the time."

At that, Angela winced. "Apparently that was a setup between the two of them. Sadie would use Tamara as an excuse any time she wanted to go off and have some … fun."

"*Go off and have fun,*" Riff repeated in a soft and slightly menacing tone.

Angela shrugged. "I don't know what you want me to say. All I'm doing is giving you the information," she murmured. "Don't shoot the messenger. According to Tamara, my sister wasn't quite ready to settle down."

"So, what then? Marriage to me was a life sentence?" he asked, feeling stunned all over again.

"Don't forget," Angela repeated, giving him a look. "All I'm doing is passing on the message."

He quickly reined in his temper and nodded. "Anybody else have anything?"

She shook her head. "Kim also had a suspicion that another person was in Sadie's life, but she didn't know who. She was pretty upset to hear where the crime scene was. So, I guess a part of me says Kim had a bit more than suspicion, but maybe she just didn't have the ability to tell my sister to stop."

"Did anybody ever have that ability?" Riff asked moodily.

"I sure never did," Angela stated. "Anyway, that's all I've got. I called everybody who I knew were friends with Sadie back then, and that's where we're at." She looked at the files in front of them and winced. "Anything?"

Riff shook his head. "No, but we're supposed to be getting a list of known associates for Johnny Waco. And we need to find this Chip guy."

"Right, I forgot about him," Angela muttered, then took a deep breath. "I want to go with you when you talk to people."

He stared at her, understanding where she was coming from, but really hating that she would be tagging along. The trouble was, he couldn't really understand why. "It would be better if you didn't," he noted cautiously.

"Undoubtedly," she said. "Apparently a lot of my life would be better if I didn't do things," she quipped, aware that she sounded bitter and hostile. "But, in this case, just like you, I want answers."

It was hard to argue with that because now they both needed a way to resolve this enough so that they could each move forward with their lives. They needed closure of some sort, a way to put to rest something that had turned from ugly to despairingly ugly, and neither one of them could move on until it was settled.

"Fine," he said in exasperation. "It'll mean packing a bag and spending a few days in London though."

She nodded. "It'll save on the drive back-and-forth."

"It will." He looked over at Terkel, who was already nodding.

"And, of course, we'll be here on standby," Terkel confirmed, with a nod. "And, just in case you think you're going without backup, forget about it. Royce and Langdon are going with you as well."

She looked surprised and asked, "Don't they need to be working for you?"

"They *are* working for me," Terkel declared, his tone steady but refuting any argument. "Riff is part of this investigative team, and he's done a lot of good for a lot of people. So, we need to confirm that this comes to an end without anything blowing up in all our faces." He looked over at her and smiled. "Of course you get to leave, … if the women let you leave, that is."

She rolled her eyes. "Thankfully all the babies have come as planned, so, … unless you guys are anticipating another wave?" She cast him a sideways look and then burst out laughing as she noted the look of horror on his face.

"We are barring that second wave for now, and we don't need it coming anytime soon. Hopefully we should be good for a while."

"Accidents happen of course, but everybody knows that—and then some. Clary and Cara appear to be far more talented and skilled at some of this stuff than I could ever hope to be," Angela murmured. "What they can do is truly amazing."

Terk nodded. "It is, but there's a place for all kinds of medicine in the world," he added, "and you have yours."

"Maybe, but it sure makes me wonder about doing more."

"When we get this resolved, we can talk about it."

She looked at him. "What does that mean?"

"If you want to train, and you want to do more with your energy skills, you're welcome to," he stated, with a shrug. "Believe me that it hasn't escaped anybody's notice that you do energy work as easily as breathing, and that's very important to this work that we do. So, if you want to do more, to learn more, we'll talk about it, after we get this wrapped up."

She smiled. "That would be fun."

He laughed. "It is fun, but it can also be very taxing."

"Yeah, I know, but what I'm already doing is taxing anyway. I guess what I want to say is that anything that can help us get there a little quicker and heal some of these people a little faster is all good." At that, she hopped up. "I'll go get my bag." She looked over at Riff and frowned. "You won't take off without me, will you?"

The wariness in her tone had him raising his head and glaring at her. "Hey, I already said you could come," he replied with the dark tone that he seemed to have reserved just for her. "Just don't expect me to look after you."

She snorted and shook her head. "Of course not. That would be far too much to ask for." And, with that, she turned and walked out.

He slumped back and glared at Terkel. "What am I supposed to say? It's not as if I'm the least bit comfortable around her."

"No, but maybe you should look at *why* you're not comfortable around her," Terkel suggested with a smile, as he got up in a lazy motion. "You might be surprised at the answer."

"Maybe I don't want to look," he muttered to himself, but Terkel caught it.

He turned at the doorway, his face alight with amusement. "I'm sure you don't, and yet, when this is over, … you should probably take a really close look at *why*."

And, with that, he was gone, leaving Riff sitting there, wondering.

CHAPTER 7

WHEN ANGELA AND Riff pulled into London and soon were parked at a hotel, Angela turned to Riff. "So Langdon and Royce will join us later?"

Riff nodded. "As needed."

She asked, "Did the team book us ahead of time?"

"They did."

She smiled because, all the way on this drive, Riff had been unexpectedly friendly. Cautious but friendly, and she appreciated that. If they could get through this process, then maybe there would be hope for at least an amicable future between them. She didn't dare hope for more than that, not while he was still so furiously angry with her.

Maybe that was enough for her. Maybe it wasn't a good thing to care as much as she did. Her sister certainly thought it was funny, and that just smarted even more. Angela had tried hard to forget the hateful words Sadie had spouted the last time Angela had seen her sister, but they kept rearing their ugly heads on a regular basis. It just reminded her that, even though her sister was gone, her influence was not.

"We already have a room, and we're registered."

"Oh good. So, we just have to pick up the keys?"

He nodded and walked over to the front desk, spoke with management at the reception desk for a moment, was handed the keys, and he came back to her. With a smile, he noted, "Second floor."

"Is the second floor good?"

"Yeah, it is," he confirmed. "Much easier to avoid people coming in when you don't want them to."

She winced at that. "I would have thought the ground floor was better because then you would have an easy exit."

"Second floor is pretty easy for exits too," he noted, "but much harder for people to get at you."

"God," she muttered. "Not exactly what I wanted to hear."

"Maybe not," he conceded, "but, in this instance, I don't know whether we're safe or not."

"I wanted to ask about that. So you're worried about somebody coming after us?"

"It's certainly something to bear thinking about, isn't it?" he asked.

She nodded. "A lot of people were involved, and how many have turned up dead?"

"A lot," he replied, clearly agreeing with her. "The question is, does anybody give a shit *now* that we're not dead, and is there any reason for them to try and take us out?"

"Is there?" she asked, as she studied him. "I wasn't thinking that we were in danger here, at least not beyond the norm."

"When you say, *beyond the norm*, what does that mean?" he asked curiously, as he walked to their hotel room door, unlocked it, and pushed it open so she could enter.

"I don't know. I guess I wasn't really thinking that far ahead," she admitted. "I've been so focused on getting through this, so I wasn't really analyzing my emotions or thought processes too coherently."

He laughed. "Yeah, we noticed."

She glared at him but walked in and realized they had a suite with adjoining rooms. "Is this wise?" she asked, pointing at the rooms.

"Yeah," he replied, with that same nonchalant tone. "Better to be together in case anything does happen, than to be apart and not able to find you."

"Right. What happened to that whole *I'm not looking after you* thing?"

"Yeah, well, that lasted all of five minutes, and I realized I couldn't do that to your sister."

She sucked in her breath and turned away from him, just so he couldn't see the pain in her face. "That makes sense," she managed to get out, as she quickly chose one of the bedrooms and went inside, closing the door behind her. She leaned against the door and closed her eyes. The last thing she wanted was him looking after her as some debt to her dead, lying, cheating sister. Angela definitely didn't want to die in the process of investigating her sister's murder, but, damn, Riff's motivation to protect Angela only because of Sadie was tough to swallow. Partly because Angela was damn sure her sister would have preferred otherwise. Taking several deep breaths to center herself, she eventually headed into the en suite bathroom, where she quickly refreshed herself by washing her face and brushing her hair.

The trip had been long and awkward, more so because they were studiously avoiding discussing anything that would risk setting off all their rampant emotions again. When she walked back out to the common room, Riff was slouched on the couch, working on his laptop. "I'll need food," she stated briskly.

He looked up and nodded. "Me too. You want to go out or order in?"

She pondered that. "I wouldn't mind getting out for a little fresh air at this point."

"Good enough," he replied, as he put down his laptop and got up.

"I can go alone," she suggested hesitantly. "Bring you back something?"

But he shook his head. "No way, not happening. While we're in this, we're in this together. I can't take the chance of anything happening to you right now." She considered arguing against that but decided staying quiet might be the best recourse. "Give me a minute," he said, then turned and headed to his room.

She sat down beside the laptop, wondering if she should look at what he was researching, then realized it was probably better if she didn't. Some things were painful, and the details of her sister's crime scene had been rough in the beginning. She couldn't imagine that this *motel as a crime scene investigation* would have been any easier. Not that she knew that's what he'd been doing, but somehow it's what she thought Riff might have been looking at.

When he came out and looked at his laptop, with her seated nearby, he zeroed in on her. "Did you look?"

"No, I didn't," she said. "I was afraid it was something I didn't want to see."

He nodded in understanding. "You don't. ... You really don't." With that, he picked up his laptop and took it into his room. When he came out, he added, "Come on. Let's go." As they stepped out into the hallway and walked toward the stairs, he asked, "What are you craving for food?"

"Anything. Just fresh air and food of almost any kind would be good. It's been a very long day already."

"It'll seem to be a very long week at the rate we're going," he noted, walking down the stairs beside her. "Or maybe just make it a very long year."

She nodded. "It's funny," she began, "because I kept waiting and hoping that something in the case would break, that there would be answers. Then, when that happened, it was way harder to deal with than I ever expected. I just want it to all go away, not to stir up all those ugly thoughts and images again." She stopped talking as they crossed the foyer toward the front door.

He didn't say anything but nodded in understanding.

"Have you dealt with death very much?" she asked, surprised at herself, because she really didn't want to talk about this at all. Yet she couldn't seem to stop herself from bringing it up.

He looked at her and shrugged. "Too much as far as I'm concerned. It's not as if you haven't in your work either, right?"

"Yeah. Still, although they were patients who ripped me up on the inside when we lost them, in a way they were more distant, a lot easier to deal with than this."

"It's family in this case," he pointed out. "And, when it's family, all bets are off."

She smiled, happy that at least they were talking somewhat naturally. As they stepped outside, she stopped and sniffed the air and smiled. "This helps."

"We could have stopped on the trip and walked around a little bit," he noted, eyeing her curiously. "I didn't realize you were getting claustrophobic."

"I wasn't," she stated, turning to him. "It's just nice to know that the trip is over and that we're on to whatever is ahead of us. It will be what it is, although I just realized I don't even know what the plan is," she muttered.

"Yet you still couldn't help but get involved," he pointed out.

Only this time, a wry note of understanding filled his tone, not mockery or disgust. "I need to be there, even at the end."

He nodded. "I get it, but what's really messed up is that we were both betrayed by the same woman, and yet we're standing here for her, ... even though she hurt us both."

"I think that *because* she hurt us both, we each need to say goodbye in whatever way makes sense to us," she shared. "I want to move on, without feeling guilty that she didn't get the chance to live out her life naturally. Plus, I want to move on without hearing the nastiness of her voice in my head and all the horrid things she said to me. I don't know how to put those to rest until she is put to rest. It's almost as if, by listening to those words right now, I help keep her alive just so I can help solve this."

He went quiet for a long time as they walked at a slow and steady pace down the street.

She looked at a few of the restaurant fronts, trying to figure out what she wanted to eat. Yet it wasn't even so much that she was hungry, as much as she just wanted to get out, to move around, and to get some fresh air.

When he stopped in front of an Indian restaurant, he looked at her. "I've been in this one before."

"Was it any good?" she asked.

"It was," he replied in a casual tone. "Are you up for Indian though?"

"Sure, why not?" she said agreeably. When they went in, they were given a table. As she sat down, she asked curiously, "Were you here with my sister?"

He shook his head. "No. It's funny you ask because I

was wondering if I was just away so much on assignments that I didn't do enough things like this with her."

"Yet, if you'd asked her about your life together, what would she have said?"

"She would have said she was good. She was always telling me to go off and save the world, as if that was what I was doing," he noted, a self-mocking grin on his face. "And, sure, I was working on missions and various jobs, helping people all around the world, but she never seemed to mind."

He shook his head, as if laughing at his own stupidity. "This is so stupid. For the longest time I thought I was the luckiest man in the world because I had a fiancée who understood how I felt compelled to do this, who really got how important it was that I get out there and do these jobs. Yet, according to what I've learned now, either she was getting rid of me or she was dealing with what I was asking of her. And she didn't know how to say anything different."

"She knew exactly how to say something different," Angela declared. "Sadie was never shy about voicing her opinion."

He laughed at that. "No, she wasn't," he agreed, with a knowing smile. "She usually gave as good as she got too."

At that, Angela laughed and nodded. It was unusual to talk with him about her sister and to not be ripping into each other or hurting each other because of it. "It does bring a measure of peace," she muttered. "I know it sounds foolish, but even just finding *where* she died and possibly *why* she was there makes a difference. I get that maybe it makes it worse for you, but it makes it easier for me."

He studied her for a long time and then nodded. "I can certainly see how it would be easier for you," he shared, "because it validates what you already knew. For me, hearing all that for the first time, well, it hasn't been easy. Yet, in some ways, it does make some of her actions fall into place."

He sighed and continued. "Quite a few times, when I wanted to go out and do things or wanted her to come up to London and to spend a few days with me, she wouldn't. She was always busy with friends and people and events. I don't even know what things, but it seemed as if whatever she was involved in took precedence. At the time, I just went about my business and smiled, feeling good because I'd been trying to be a good partner, and she seemed totally okay with the fact that I just wasn't around."

Riff shared it all dispassionately, and it sounded alien to Angela.

Then he sighed. "I should have heard the warning bells. I see that now. I should have realized that, while people can be understanding to a certain extent, she had taken it to the extreme."

"That's an interesting thought," Angela noted. "I hadn't considered that."

"I've had a few hours to consider what I do know, and, as hard as it is to put the pieces together, they are finally getting there, and, for that," he said, looking around the restaurant first, "I owe you an apology for attacking you yesterday."

She shook her head vehemently. "No, you don't. If I could have found a way to tell you, I would have, but there was no way that I could tell you anything about what Sadie was up to without it coming across in a horrible way, and I just wasn't up for that. And I wasn't up for analyzing or dissecting her actions any further. I was still hurting myself," she shared. "I haven't talked to my ex-fiancé since." When he looked at her in surprise, she shrugged and added, "He didn't want to talk about it."

"He didn't even try to see you again?"

She shook her head. "Nope, apparently he fell head over heels in love with Sadie and couldn't help himself, *blah, blah, blah*, and, had I been more like her, then he would have loved me more."

"Oh, ouch. Yeah, that's not exactly what you want to hear, is it?"

"No, not when I found them in bed, not when I'm already listening to my sister bash me for being less than what I was supposed to be," she explained, with a sarcastic laugh. "So, I just took it to mean that my ex and I were obviously not good together to begin with, and it was time to call it quits, but it still wasn't easy. I went through quite a crisis at the time, and then Sadie, … well, she was killed soon afterward."

He just nodded.

When the waiter came around, Riff asked her, "Do you know what you want to order?"

She shook her head, clearly at a loss. "No. If you have an idea, please just go ahead and choose for me."

He quickly ordered for the two of them, and the waiter took off, happy to have somebody who apparently knew what he was after. Riff turned back to her. "Did you ever talk to Sadie about it again?"

She shrugged. "Not a whole lot to talk about. She'd been caught right in the middle of it and admitted to it. Obviously because … I found them in bed together," she pointed out. "Sadie thought it was funny as hell, and we didn't speak afterward. That's part of the guilt. What if I had talked to her? What if I had reached out? What if I had … I don't know." She stared off in the distance.

Riff sighed. "I don't think there are any more *what-ifs* that we can do anything about because obviously your ex-fiancé wasn't the only man in Sadie's life, since she had also hooked up with this Johnny Waco right away. So maybe that's something we both need to acknowledge too. For whatever reason, Sadie felt she wanted and needed to do this, and she did it, not appearing to care whom she hurt in the process."

Angela sat here, stunned at his calm analysis.

"And while we're the ones who were hurt in the process, Sadie was the one who paid the ultimate price," he pointed out. "So, if we can come to terms with that and can move on, maybe we can leave her in peace."

She stared at him, almost open-mouthed. "Wow." Angela sat in silence, not really knowing what to say to that. "You've only just found out, and yet, here you are, already handling it so much better than I am."

He frowned at her and shook his head. "I didn't mean it that way at all," he countered. "I'm not diminishing what she did or how I feel about it, and I've got a lot of soul searching to do there. I'm just saying that, if the two of us can find a way forward, it would make our lives a little easier."

She nodded. "I'm certainly not arguing that point, and God knows I want to find an easier way forward. You and I have been at loggerheads for a very long time."

He gave her a ghost of a smile. "We're on the course to solve this thing, so, with any luck, … maybe lots of problems could be solved."

She wasn't sure what that meant, but she was willing to accept what appeared to be something of a peace offering. She hesitated for a long moment.

He looked over at her. "You look as if you're trying to

say something but don't really know if you can. I promise that I'm a whole lot calmer about the whole thing now."

A crooked smile slipped out. "I'm glad you are, but I'm not so sure that I am. It's all brought up a lot of anger again."

"And with good reason," he agreed. "I'm sorry she did that. You seemed to be so excited about the fiancé."

"Yeah, well, then you learn that it's not real and that I apparently wasn't good enough after all," she said in a mocking tone.

He winced at that. "Only as I think about it now do I realize Sadie had quite a habit of sending digs at you, didn't she?"

She laughed. "Yeah, but most of the time it didn't matter. I just knew she did that because she had to be so very unhappy."

"And yet," he replied, staring at her, not quite in fascination but with a questioning expression, "how is it that she wasn't happy, and yet we were engaged? I mean, why were we engaged if it's not what she wanted? Why were we engaged at all?" he asked in bewilderment. "Apparently I didn't know anything about her."

She winced. "I'm sorry. I didn't mean to dredge that all up again too."

"We'll be doing this a lot," he noted, "tripping over each other's feelings and emotions. Plus, we'll both be a bit of a wreck for a while, and that's okay too. *Patience.*"

She laughed. "*Right*, patience."

Just then the waiter came with their dishes and set them on the table. She inhaled the sharp curry aroma and smiled. "It smells delicious," she shared to the waiter, thanking him. He just smiled and quickly disappeared.

They both dug into the food, and then she looked up at him quizzically. "One thing she told me I never quite understood."

"What's that?" he asked, looking up from his dish, even as he scooped up some of the fresh hot curry.

"That she was never waiting for you to come home."

He nodded. "I know. I joked about it one time, how she didn't seem to care if I came or went, and she took offense, saying that she just aired her feelings differently. I hope that she at least cared for me. I hope that my being there was something that she wanted, but trust me. I'm going through my own crisis of thoughts, wondering if she ever even gave a damn. Like, was I just a cover for something else? Did I and my career give her permission to go off and to live the life that she really wanted? I don't know," he muttered, with a shake of his head. "And, I suspect at this point, we may never know."

"And that's the hard part, isn't it?" she murmured.

Just then his phone rang. He pulled it out, looked at the screen, and said, "Sorry. I better take this. It's Jonas."

In a low voice, he answered the call, looking around to see if anybody else was close enough to hear. Then something important was shared because Riff put down his fork ever-so-slowly, whispering to her, "Hang on a minute. I'll take this outside. Stay here."

And, with that, he got up and walked out, leaving her alone in the restaurant, watching him leave.

"OKAY, JONAS, I'M outside. What's going on?" What he heard next caught him by surprise. "What?"

He listened as Jonas explained how James, the prisoner they had gone to see, had been murdered in prison. "Shit," Riff muttered, shaking his head. "He was nervous about it and lobbying for better accommodations, but we had no idea that talking to us would get him killed. I still don't understand what's behind it."

"The only thing I can see," Jonas replied, his tone harsh, "is that whoever wanted James dead may have been the third person at that motel or, even more likely, your fiancée's killer. He's got something to hide and is doing an awful lot to confirm he doesn't get caught. We also haven't found anyone named Chip connected to Johnny Waco."

"And, of course, we have that third person's DNA but can't seem to find a match for him. Possibly the Chip who James mentioned, but we still don't know who Chip is."

"Exactly." Jonas took a moment and added, "So now you don't have to worry about him getting moved to a better facility. It also stops us from having him as a witness in the event this goes to trial."

"Angela will be pretty upset about it."

"I'm sure," Jonas replied. "So, you tell her any way you want to. Better you than me." And, with that, he rang off.

Riff stood outside, watching the world pass by for a long moment. Then he headed back inside and sat down across from her.

"What's the matter?" she asked, taking a sip of her tea.

Glancing around the room, Riff looked over at her and whispered, "Remember the prisoner who gave us the information?"

She nodded, and then she froze, as if she already knew. She leaned forward. "Is he dead?"

He nodded. "Yeah, he was found hanging in his cell overnight."

Her eyes widened, as if the information wasn't quite what she'd expected.

"And, yes, they suspect foul play," he murmured.

"Oh, good Lord." She groaned. "So telling us that information really did get him killed."

"It's certainly possible, but we're not sure about that, so let's not jump to conclusions. That also doesn't mean we are out of danger ourselves, and that's one reason why Jonas called. On the off chance that somebody knows we visited James, Jonas wanted to remind us to take it easy and to watch our backs."

"Which we'll do anyway," she murmured, "but now it's even more important."

"Absolutely," he agreed, looking around casually. "So, let's eat up and get back to the hotel."

She winced, stared down at her food, and quickly dug in, even though she had lost her appetite. He followed suit. When they were done, he dropped enough money on the table to make everybody happy and rushed her outside.

"You moved me out of there damn fast."

"Yep, I sure did. I'm not feeling very good about any of this right now."

"But even if somebody did know we were at the per-hour motel or at the prison, which I gather they can find out pretty easily," she noted, "it still doesn't mean that they know we're in London right now."

"They could have tracked us from the prison, back to Terkel's, and now here again, also noting our license plate."

That put it all together for her, and she cried out, "Holy shit. We brought the same vehicle too, didn't we?"

"We did," he confirmed grimly. "And, right about now, I wish we hadn't."

CHAPTER 8

BACK AT THE hotel, Angela paced with uneasy energy, as Riff talked to the rest of the team by phone. She didn't contribute anything to the call on Speakerphone, but she still appreciated being included because that allowed her to stay in the loop. This new information definitely added a whole different element to their situation.

"We're on our way to join you," Langdon shared. "We held off, wondering if there would be a change in location, but we'll grab a suite in the same hotel tonight. You'll need backup."

"We won't be leaving this hotel room anytime soon," Riff shared, "and we need intel as to who could have been involved in this latest guy's murder. Specifically, was it possible to hire from outside the prison or if somebody inside the prison got worried?"

"It was probably a for-hire job from somebody outside the prison, yet using an inmate or even a guard to carry out the order," Terkel noted. "Jonas called me earlier, and we discussed some options, and that one came up. As far as the energy at the prison or as to the whole scenario, all I can tell you is that everything feels wrong."

"Yeah, I got that much already," Riff replied, struggling to keep his tone calm.

Angela walked over, placed a hand on his shoulder, and

sent some soothing energy down his back. She was not sure how effective that was, until he took a deep breath and let it go, relaxing almost immediately.

He smiled up at her and nodded his thanks.

She went back to pacing, not even sure what else to do. There had to be something, but right now it seemed as if they were sitting ducks. She hated to think that James—who had just been trying to do something better in his life—was dead now too.

She wished there had been a message from Sadie that would have revealed what was going on. But, if there was, it would also mean that her sister could have easily been involved in something really ugly, and that was just one more thing they didn't really want to confirm. To find out her sister was having affairs with criminals in cheap motels, probably just for the thrill of it, was bad enough. Yet to find out that she may have been a criminal herself? Angela had a hard time considering that.

But what if Sadie knew something about all this?

Angela pondered that, and, when Riff got off the phone, she asked him, "Did you go through all of Sadie's personal stuff after her death?"

He looked at her, then shrugged. "We were living together, but I still felt odd about going through her belongings. So I just put everything in storage. I checked it all over as I boxed it but not with an eye as to what we know now." She stared at him steadily, and he winced. "Are you thinking we need to take a look at that storage locker?"

"I do," she agreed. "We don't know what this is all about, but obviously more is here than we realize, even now. So, it's hard to consider or to bypass anything."

"You're right," he muttered, sitting back and staring at

her. "I should have thought of it myself."

She laughed. "We haven't had two seconds to think of anything," she noted. "It's just been chaos from one minute to the next. Nobody expects you to have all the answers, you know? We also have not been utilizing any energy skills, and, if there is energy that we could utilize, it would certainly help."

"It sure would," he stated, "and you're right. I haven't been utilizing energy to the utmost. I did see vestiges of her energy in the motel room, which surprised me, as it's been so long. But that speaks to the violence at the time and to the amount of blood shed at the scene. There isn't necessarily anything there to track or follow, but, as I think about it, logistically speaking, we should go to the locker."

"Let's go now then." She jumped to her feet. When he just stared at her, she shrugged. "We're sitting ducks here anyway. I would feel better if we did something."

"I would feel better if we had backup before we headed out on nighttime prowls," he added. "Plus, I'm not sure the storage lockers are even open at this hour."

"Oh, I never thought of that."

He chuckled. "I'm glad that we've got a plan for something to do, some avenue to pursue tomorrow, but let's confirm that it's at least morning when we do it."

She groaned. "So, now I'm supposed to relax and sleep like a log, right?"

"That would help, and, if you can't, then you can't," he said. "Anything you can do to get some rest would be helpful."

She nodded. "In that case I'll have a shower and try to crash." She checked her watch and winced. "Damn, it's later than I thought." With that, she headed off to her bedroom.

After she was showered and curled up in bed with a book, she found it almost impossible to read. She reviewed everything going on and knew that no way could Riff be asleep either. She hopped out of bed and walked out to the living room, finding him sitting there, nursing a drink. "I can't sleep," she announced. "Did you bring alcohol with you?" she asked, staring at him.

He pointed to the small side table. "Help yourself."

She walked over and poured herself a healthy drink. "Don't mind if I do. If nothing else, maybe it'll help me sleep."

"If it does, great, but I don't think anything'll help me sleep," he muttered.

"Still feeling guilty?"

"I don't know if *guilt* is the right word," he said, "but, yeah, I'm definitely still feeling messed-up over it all, and I probably will for a while."

"Yeah, I can see that. At least we're getting somewhere."

"Says you," he muttered, as he glared at her. "I guess I need to tell you that, no matter how I hard I try, I'm still struggling with the fact that you didn't tell me."

"Struggle away then," she snapped, as she picked up the glass and walked back toward her bedroom, knowing that there was absolutely no point in staying out there with him if it wouldn't be productive. It appeared he was back to being the senseless twit she was so used to by now.

She turned at her doorway and spat, "The thing is, you weren't there, and I was still dealing with my own after-shocks. So, deal with it yourself on your own time because I really don't have the time or the energy to deal with your stuff too."

And, with that, she slammed the door and proceeded to go to sleep.

RIFF WOKE THE next morning, nursing one hell of a headache. He groaned, knowing that drinking that much was one of the stupidest things he could have done, but, hell, his world had been full of stupid things over the last few days. And, for him, normally so good at finding things and people, he was struggling with the fact that he hadn't known, hadn't seen any of what was going on with Sadie. Therefore, he was forced to deal with all of it now.

It made no sense to him that he hadn't known before. Then he had to wonder if Sadie might have used energy to hide what she was doing. He pondered that as he showered and got dressed. When he came out to the living room, Angela sat there, staring at him.

He raised an eyebrow. "Did you get any sleep at all?"

"No," she declared flatly. "A little rough to get sleep amid all this."

He nodded. "Let me ask you something. Did your sister utilize energy?"

"Yes. I told you that before." He didn't say anything. "Now you don't believe me about that either?" she asked, with a tone of disgust. "What makes you question it?"

"I just wondered," he clarified in an agreeable tone of voice. "Again, I'm still dealing with the fact that I didn't know anything was wrong, and I'm trying to understand how that could be."

"Sadie might have used energy for that then."

He slowly turned and looked at her.

She shrugged. "I do remember Sadie saying something about having a way to hide shit. I just didn't realize that her way of hiding things was to hurt those around her."

"Do you know what she could do with energy?"

"Sure, she would tell you that everything was okay and make you feel fine, didn't she?"

"Yes, of course. I told you that."

"*That* was energy. It was her way of making sure that everything was fine and that she could go off and do her own thing." He sat down hard and stared at her. She shrugged. "I get it, and I don't like it either. I didn't like it when she tried to do it with me."

"She tried it?"

"Yeah, she did. It was part of that whole *screwing around with my fiancé* thing," she reminded him. "When I realized it, I told her just what I thought of somebody who would utilize energy in that way. She just laughed and told me that … I was a stick in the mud, and I needed to get real. There was so much else in life, and I should just let it go."

"Just let it go," he repeated, staring at her.

"Yeah, that was Sadie's way of dealing with anything, apparently," she replied. "I couldn't let it go of course. How do you see the breakup of your relationship as just *let it go*, all because somebody needed a thrill in her life?" She winced, realizing how bitter she still felt. "Here we go, bouncing off each other again."

"Yes, but you're right," he admitted. "I was just thinking that too, how she must have used energy on me. I've been looking for a reason to explain why I didn't know, why I couldn't have found out about her affairs. Now I do want to believe that she did something to hide it from me, but that's still no excuse. It still doesn't change the fact that I should have known," he stated in disgust. "I guess I didn't really want to know."

"No, you didn't want to know," she confirmed, "any

more than I did. Do you know how stupid I felt when I realized the relationship between Sadie and my fiancé had been going on for weeks if not months?"

He stared at her and swallowed hard. "God, Sadie really played us, didn't she?"

"Yeah, she sure did," Angela declared bitterly. Then she winced and closed her eyes. "It's all right, you know?"

"Is it?"

"It's my sister. I should love her, forgive her, right?"

"Maybe for yourself, if for no other reason, and one day you probably will, but nobody said it had to be today."

She let out her breath. "I need coffee."

"Yeah, you and me both." Just then his phone buzzed. He checked his cell and shared, "The guys are downstairs and want to go out for food."

"Good," she said, brightening. She appeared to be flagging in spirit and energy. "I could do with some food." And, with that, moments later they were headed out to meet up with the rest of the team in the parking lot. With her at his side, they walked closer to Langdon and Royce only to have her look around in alarm, "It just feels so weird to me."

"In what way?" he asked.

She stopped. "The whole set up feels weird. I don't know how to explain it."

"You're doing pretty good though, considering, so keep it up."

She shrugged and added, "I hate to say it, but I guess I'm wondering if Johnny Waco wasn't just a casual fling for her, and something more was to it."

"Yeah, I'm wondering the same," Riff shared, "and yet it would have been on the heels of your ex, right?"

"Not really. The way Sadie talked, my ex was just one of

many, and yet she had somebody special in her life, but she wasn't sure what to do about him. At the time I thought she meant you."

"I'm pretty sure we can both assume at this point that I was the last person she thought about in that way," he declared in a brutally honest tone. "I was a means to a comfortable lifestyle and no strings to tie her down, apparently."

"It just would have been nice if she had told us first."

"Exactly."

As they walked out to the car, Langdon and Royce were there, waiting for them. She lifted a hand in greeting.

They had smiles on their faces. "You guys up for some breakfast?"

"We definitely need coffee if nothing else," she shared with a smile, glancing around and considering their choices. "Breakfast would be good too."

A black truck drove past them, and gunfire erupted.

CHAPTER 9

ANGELA WAS FLUNG to the ground and covered by a hot, heavy body, as the vehicle revved its engine and took off, spraying gravel behind. She groaned, and the weight was removed, as Riff looked around, then stood up and helped her to her feet. "Is it safe?" she asked.

"It is at the moment," he murmured, nodding at Langdon and Roy. They were both fine but shaken. She sighed. "I guess they know where we are now."

"Yeah, you're not kidding." Riff stared in the direction the vehicle went. "The question is who?"

"Did anybody see anything?" she asked.

Langdon nodded. "I got a couple letters from the license plate," he replied, as he pulled out his phone. "I'll update Terkel on this one."

"Yeah, we need to," Riff noted, "and I'll phone Jonas. Obviously we need more intel and fast because these guys know who and where we are, while we don't have a clue about them," he spat, fury building in his tone.

Angela frowned. "But the only way they know who we are is if they have been keeping tabs on us since our trip to the prison."

Riff nodded.

She asked, "So, where are they getting that information from?"

"It's not that hard," Royce noted, from behind them. "That information is easy to get. The question is, did they utilize help from inside the prison as a trigger, or did they just happen to consider the fact that maybe this James buddy of theirs would squawk on them?"

"Maybe both," she suggested, "and maybe we're just out of time." When they looked at her, she shrugged. "This is as active a case as we'll ever get, so we all know we need to get these assholes now because, once this evidence gets buried, potentially with us," she added, "it'll never resurface, and we'll never get the final answers. I want justice for my sister, and I want to put this whole thing to rest forever."

In a move that surprised her, she was urged into Langdon's vehicle, and they drove off so fast that she hardly realized Riff wasn't with them, not until she turned to look behind to see Riff standing there, staring after her. "We shouldn't have left him," she cried out.

"He's coming," Langdon stated.

"And where is Royce?" she asked.

"We have to divide and conquer, so, right now, we need to confirm you're safe. Thus, Royce stayed with him."

"Me?" she asked, raising her hands in frustration. "It's hardly all about me."

"Maybe it's not all about you," Langdon conceded, as he glanced at her, "yet it is."

"We were gonna head out to a storage locker Riff has for a lot of Sadie's stuff," she shared. "I wanted to search through it to confirm nothing suspicious was in it." When he frowned at her, she shrugged. "My sister was a lot of things, and a bit of a pack rat was one of them. Some might call her a hoarder."

"Interesting. I didn't even know there was a locker."

"Riff just told me about it last night," she added. "We planned to get coffee and then head up there."

"Sounds as if something we will all do together then. If there's a locker, and it happens to have any relevant information in it—"

"Exactly," she stated, with a nod.

"We need to get there before these assholes have any idea."

"For all I know, nothing is there, but—"

"We can't take the chance," he added agreeably, as he pulled into a coffee shop. "Come on. Let's go in and order for everybody."

Following his lead, she got out and headed inside. She excused herself to use the washroom, and, when she came back out, Riff and Royce were just walking in. Riff looked over at her and smiled. She raced over to him, and he opened his arms and gave her a quick hug.

"Are you okay?" he asked in concern.

She nodded. "I'm fine. I just wasn't expecting to be shot at," she explained nervously.

"No, none of us were, and yet I guess we should have been, since we found out our informant died in prison."

"I still wasn't thinking anybody would care about us."

"Obviously, James had valuable information."

"And yet is that what he gave us?" she asked. "Or did he fail to tell us something, and now we'll never know?"

"Yes, I think so, but maybe he didn't even realize what he knew. I do have a couple messages on my phone from him that didn't say anything, but now we need to sit down and listen to them again."

"From James?" she asked.

"Yeah. You gave him our numbers," he reminded her.

She nodded. When they took their seats at the table, he pulled out his phone and played the messages. The prisoner's voice was nervous as hell.

"Look. I probably shouldn't be calling, but this guy is big. He's bigger than he should be, more powerful, and he's dangerous. He's connected to the mob. I want out of here, and I need out of here fast."

And his second message was just more complaining about how long they were taking to get him out of there.

"Jesus," she muttered. "Just hearing all that makes me feel terrible. We should have helped him."

"And yet it's not your fault," Royce stated.

"No, it isn't, but we couldn't get him moved fast enough. What if we had? He would still be alive."

"Maybe. Maybe not," Riff said, frowning at her. "You don't know what else he might have done in his life or who else he may have pissed off. I can't imagine it's just a single offense that sent him to prison. For all you know, he's been blackmailing the murderer himself."

"Oh, shit." She stared at Riff in shock. "That would get him killed for sure, wouldn't it?"

"It absolutely would," he stated. "Whether James believed it or not, once you start pulling a tiger's tail, that tiger has a habit of turning around and grabbing your throat."

"But we don't know that for sure, do we?"

"No, we don't know anything for sure," Riff declared. "What I do know is, I want to head to this locker to confirm nothing's there, while we wait for people running an APB to track down that drive-by vehicle. You can bet an awful lot more cops are picking up an interest as to what we're doing now."

"Particularly Jonas," Royce said, with a smile. "He

doesn't want to lose us. We're doing his bottom line too much good."

She frowned at him and asked, "You guys do a lot of work for him, don't you?"

He nodded. "Terkel does, and those of us who have joined the team are all heavily invested in MI6. So, yeah, we're an asset they don't want to lose," Royce stated. "This won't help their reputation either."

"Yet nobody would know the difference," she pointed out. "I wouldn't have known MI6 was involved at all."

"No, most people don't. It's not what their mandate deals with. I'm sure Jonas moved quickly in order to not have himself get taken off the case," Royce added. "That's another aspect to this that most people don't really understand. This thing can't continue. All kinds of repercussions fall on budgets and teams. People don't take it kindly when you start shooting operatives."

"Yet you guys aren't exactly operatives," she clarified, with a glance at them.

"No, not exactly. We're just, … shall we say, *private*. Members of the very elite club."

She laughed. "It's as good a word as any, but it still doesn't really tell us anything."

"No, and that's the whole point of it," Royce declared, with a chuckle. "Private is as private does."

"Again, words that don't mean anything."

He grinned and nodded. "Nope."

She sighed. "Okay, so breakfast and then to the storage locker. We'll just ignore the shooting for now, right?"

Riff shook his head. "We won't ignore the drive-by. We need to stay close together. At least, if they try to hit one of us, they'll be aiming for all four of us. We'll have a four-times-better chance of getting them first."

"First," she repeated, frowning at him, hating the memories of the shooting she had just lived through. "It would be great if we didn't have to see them at all."

He nodded. "That's the plan. Just stay close, and we'll get to the bottom of it."

As it was, breakfast was a rushed affair. They ate with purpose. Nobody spoke, and then they headed out toward the storage unit. Riff parked outside his unit, hopped out, opened the combination lock, and pulled open the door.

It was one of the smaller lockers, and inside she saw a mishmash of things. She stared in astonishment. "You really kept all this?"

He shrugged. "Yeah, I didn't know what else to do with it, so it's just been sitting here all this time."

"Maybe not today but, sometime in the near future, it's time to do some spring cleaning," she muttered.

"Good, I'm glad you volunteered to help," he replied cheerfully.

"I did no such thing."

"You need to," he noted, "as this is all your sister's shit."

"*Great*," she muttered, as she grabbed a box and brought it outside in the daylight, where it was easier to see. She asked the guys to move several more, and soon they had them on the tailgate, where it was easier to sort through the contents. It didn't take long for her to sort through and to see anything of value or interest. She rummaged through many boxes, as the men moved them out, then back in again after she'd gone through them. Then she caught sight of a small burgundy book. After a quick look inside, she quickly propped it opened and flipped through the pages to see what else was inside. A few pages in, she froze, her gaze flashing across the page in disbelief. Very quickly she turned to Riff and said, "You'll want to see this."

He stared at her. "Will I though?"

She winced. "No, but you need to."

He groaned and stepped forward. "What have you got?"

"What I've got is her diary, several volumes in fact, including the last couple weeks of her life."

He looked at them as if they were a viper about to bite him. He glanced at her, then back at the collection of diaries. "You better read them then. I don't want to." And, with that, he turned and walked away.

She stared down at the one she held, looked at Royce and Langdon, and they nodded at her. "That's something for you to do," Langdon confirmed, "but do it now while we're standing here."

"*Great,*" she muttered, "no pressure."

"We'll continue in here. You get comfortable in the back seat and just read." And that's what she did. Reading her sister's words in her diaries was beyond painful. Sometimes full of anger, as Sadie spouted out about not being able to have children, sometimes with joy, as in an almost confiding tone, where she whispered about having an affair with her sister's fiancé.

Occasionally Sadie's words suggested remorse. *I know I shouldn't be doing this, but it's like a drug. An addictive drug that says I can do this and that nobody knows, nobody cares.* Another time she wrote, *Nobody knows, and I can do whatever I want. It's like having a completely different life, a secret life that no one knows about. It's exhilarating.* The diaries were full of it.

I've never used energy this way before, but it's almost addictive. Maybe it's too addictive, and maybe it's hurting me. I don't know. I don't have anybody to talk to about it. But to know that I can fool even Riff into believing that everything is fine is powerful. And it is fine because, damn, I'm doing everything I want to do, and he has no clue. Even my sister, she has no idea of such fun, yet I feel like such a bitch.

After going back and reading that passage a second time, Angela stopped and stared off in the distance. "You felt like such a bitch, but you couldn't stop, could you?" She read on and came to realize that her sister was using a technique that she had learned to help people forget what she was doing. So, as soon as they brought up a subject, she would pat their hand and would use energy to confuse their memories of what was going on. Angela pondered that for a long moment, then she phoned Clary.

"Clary," she began, when the woman answered, "when you did your healing work on me the other night, it made me think of something. I am reading my sister's diaries right now. We found them in a storage locker, and she, … my sister, talks about a technique that she learned online, using her hands to confuse memories."

Clary sucked in her breath. "Yes, there are definitely groups like that out there," she noted, with some despair, "and, yes, it is definitely possible to do that."

"Sadie seemed addicted to knowing that she could do anything she wanted and that nobody could stop her because they weren't aware of this. She managed to talk to all of us, to manipulate all of us, and yet not one of us knew what she was doing."

"You would have known on a certain level," Clary clarified. "It's not possible to fool someone who doesn't want to be fooled. But there is a very good chance that she *was* manipulating all of you to the point that she could do whatever she wanted to do." She took a moment and asked, "She really wrote it all down in her journals?"

"Yes, quite a lot of it is in here, and there's a name for it, or maybe it's just a website." When she read it off, Clary sighed.

"Yeah, we've heard of that one before," she stated in a curt tone of voice. "Sometimes they have decent people in there, but often they're just people out trying to cause trouble or trying too hard to belong to a select little group to make them feel special. Your sister did have abilities, and, when I asked you if she utilized them, you thought she didn't."

"No, I didn't. Every time we talked about using this energy for healing, she shut me down. I tried it on some of the kids, but she wouldn't help me. In fact, she used to mock me. I did wonder if she might have used them some but not to this extent. And certainly not to hurt others …" She winced. "I hate to think she used these techniques to better herself, uncaring of who she might have harmed in the process."

"She mocked you to keep you in the dark."

"*Great*," Angela replied. "More parts of my sister I didn't know about."

"And that's okay. The more you find out about this stuff, the more you'll learn. And the more you learn, the less she gets to hide away in the darkness. And maybe she understood that it wasn't a good thing for her in the end."

"She's talking here about what a bitch she'd become, how devious, yet how all of it made her feel in control, powerful, and special."

"Again," Clary noted, "that is drunk on power, the kind of power you don't want. In my experience and from what I have seen at Terkel's, that power always backfires … quite literally."

"How does that work?"

"Your energy doesn't come away clean because you're treating other people in the wrong way from an energy balance perspective," Clary explained. "It can have very damaging effects. If your sister had lived and continued to do this, it would have had quite a negative impact on her over time."

"I just wonder what that could mean *over time*," Angela noted, "because so much of this is such a shock. To even think that she could have done that to me is very hurtful."

"To you, to Riff, and possibly to all her lovers," Clary stated. "And it's possible, or even likely perhaps, that she pushed it and did it to her boyfriend or his unsavory business partners. It's something you'll need to share with the team and at least consider."

Clary made a valid point that resonated with Angela on a whole new level.

Clary continued. "At this rate you might find all kinds of reasons why she was killed. You'll have to brace yourself and prepare for what you'll hear." Clary was sympathetic, but still her words cut.

"There's already been plenty of that today," Angela shared. "To even think that my sister was intentionally doing that to me and to Riff, to the people who chose to love her? … It's just unbelievable."

"I think at this point, it's safe to say that Sadie was desperately in need of help, didn't know how to get it, and was playing her own very dangerous games, all because she didn't understand the implications of what she was doing," Clary shared. "Just keep that in perspective and don't get sucked into that same problem."

"I wasn't planning on it," Angela stated. "I just wanted to confirm if this was even possible."

"It sounds as if we're well past *possible*," Clary noted, with a light chuckle, "but listen. Nothing says Sadie couldn't have taught that to somebody else."

"Shit," Angela muttered, looking at Riff. "That would not be good."

"No, it sure wouldn't. Anyway, keep me posted." And, with that, Clary rang off.

Riff stepped closer and eyed her in concern. "What's up?" The other men stepped up behind him, and she quickly explained. Riff looked furious, and he nodded. "I've been wondering about that," he said in a harsh tone. "After the initial shock, I realized she was doing something, was up to something, especially for all of us to *not* know, and I really didn't know. I didn't think or suspect that somebody who was supposedly there for me … would ever pull a stunt like that. Shame on me." He shook his head. "Crap, this whole thing is just making me nuts."

At that, Langdon smacked him on the shoulder. "It's not about that anymore. She's paid the ultimate price, and what we must do now is figure out whether she did this to somebody who found out what she was doing and didn't much like it or whether her murder was caused by something completely different."

Royce looked around at them. "Unfortunately, if any of these unsavory guys she was meeting up with realized that she was manipulating people like that, she would have gotten a bullet in no time." Royce shook his head. "No way they could afford to have somebody like her running loose. That would be seriously bad for business."

"Unless they could control her," Riff suggested, looking over at Angela. "That would be possible."

She nodded slowly. "Maybe, but that would imply that we're dealing with an energy worker right now."

"Unfortunately," Langdon interjected, "we've come across that several times already and even here lately, so it isn't impossible. It's unfortunately quite probable."

RIFF WALKED BACK into the storage unit and pulled out the last few boxes. He didn't think there would be anything else of importance in here, but he needed something to do to keep his mind from rambling in the wrong direction, which at this moment could be any direction at all. All he could think about was Sadie's diaries. He was riding a slippery slope of discoveries today, the kind of shit where he'd been slowly learning about his fiancée, sending him into a tailspin.

Obviously he'd had a close call on that one, and yet it wasn't at all. He'd been completely misled in so many ways. He just didn't understand why. Had she been like that all the time or was it only after she realized that she couldn't have children that she went off the rails? Of course he wouldn't get any answers from Sadie, as she wasn't around to ask. She'd managed to avoid any confrontation during the time they'd been engaged, but, in his heart of hearts, he knew that she would have walked away before they got any further with their marriage plans.

And he probably would have been left stunned, trying to figure out what had happened. That's exactly what he was doing now, so it didn't seem to make a damn bit of difference.

He hefted up the last two boxes and walked outside, dumping them on the ground without saying a word. He saw the others glancing at him and then looking away. As long as they kept looking away, he was good. Only when they kept their focus on him did he get incredibly uncomfortable. Nothing was good about this scenario for any of them, but the truth had to be found, and this was what they had to do to get there. What he didn't want was anybody asking him if he was okay. He noted a dumpster off to the side. He looked at the boxes that had gone back inside, then again at the dumpster.

At that moment, he caught Angela frowning at him. He glared right back.

She shrugged. "I wanted to ask if you were okay."

He snorted. "How about you just don't?"

"Yeah, how about I just don't," she repeated with a smile, as she looked at the boxes. "Is that the last of it?"

He nodded. "Yeah, I suggest that, while we're here, we just sort through and toss whatever we don't need. Then I can just get rid of the locker." He stared at her. "The reason for keeping it seems pretty useless right now."

And, with that done, he picked up multiple boxes that had gone back inside and tossed them into the dumpster without a backward glance. The men helped. Riff walked back into the locker and double-checked that nothing remained. Nothing had fallen from the boxes, and it was a small room to check. So walking inside was more of an excuse to get away just for the moment.

As he came back out, he nodded to the others. "It's completely empty." Then he turned and locked the door again. He pulled up his phone, found the information on the storage locker, and quickly sent an email, canceling his rental agreement, effective immediately.

He still had another couple months before it automatically renewed, but, once it was empty, and he notified them about it, he wouldn't get charged for any further payments. Right about now, it was hard to even imagine how much money he'd put into this already, especially when he considered everything else that had happened. He looked over at the men. "I suggest we take this back to the hotel."

"Good call," Langdon noted, with a shrug. "That way you can go through the boxes at your leisure, not that we're expecting much, other than from the diaries."

"No, but some of her personal stuff is here," he noted, turning to Angela, "if you want any of it."

She winced and nodded. "I'll take a look."

With that, they loaded all the boxes she'd set aside to keep. Royce and Langdon pulled out first into traffic. Riff let other vehicles go ahead, prompting Angela to ask, "Do you think we were followed here?"

"I don't know," he admitted. "I'll give the guys a bit of a head start, and we'll come up behind."

She nodded.

"Do you have the diaries with you?"

"Yes. I didn't put them back in the boxes, just in case."

"And Langdon and Royce are aware that this is a *just in case* scenario too," Riff pointed out. "So they'll be watching their backs. Once you're shot at before breakfast, you're never quite relaxed anymore."

She didn't say anything but settled in beside him. As he drove off the lot, she muttered, "I know you don't want anybody to ask if you're okay, but—"

"I'm fine," he declared briskly.

"A complete change can reorient us, putting my sister in

a harsh light," she admitted. "However, I get it. It's hard to even think of her with a charitable attitude at this point," she muttered and groaned. "So why do I keep trying?"

"Keep trying," he suggested, his tone softer. "Whatever her reasons and whatever she did died with her. We must confirm that the repercussions are minimized and that we won't pay a still higher price for whatever she might have done."

"Oh, I can agree with that," Angela agreed, "but it is rough. It feels almost as if we're letting her down in a way." He looked over at her in surprise, as she shrugged. "I know. That doesn't feel very normal or right either, especially considering what we just found out, but what can I say?" She was clearly frustrated about something. "My need for answers was pretty strong, and then you find out some shadier things about it all, and thereafter you find yourself wondering why you're doing what you're doing."

"We're still after answers," Riff stated. "I still need closure. We need to find Sadie's killer. You've had a little more time to adapt to some of the information," he noted, shooting her a glance. "And, no, I'm not trying to bring up a sore topic, but—"

She nodded but kept silent.

He appreciated that. There was no easy timeline for closure. "If she had lived much longer after your big fight with Sadie, things could have been different. However, since she was killed so soon afterward, I can kind of understand why you held your peace."

She looked at him, and he ignored her searching gaze because he knew she was trying to see if forgiveness was in his apology. He wasn't entirely sure, though he figured an element of forgiveness was there. Still, he remained pissed.

Except now he didn't know if he was pissed over Sadie's actions or pissed over Angela's.

Angela added, "I guess, to you, it feels like a double betrayal in a way, doesn't it?"

He snorted. "Yeah, you could say that."

She nodded. "It's something I was dealing with myself for a long time."

"Yeah?"

"It's true. I mean, both my fiancé and my sister betrayed me five years ago," she clarified, "and then I was trying to figure out how to handle telling you in the midst of it all. I really wasn't thinking too clearly, and then, by the time she died, I was so hurt and confused that I hadn't had a chance to really consider you at all. I thought at one point that maybe it would all die with her, but, since we couldn't get any answers, nothing died," she pointed out. "It just kept dragging on and on."

"Now it'll stop," Riff declared, "because now we both can see the need for it to all go away."

"I'm sorry," she muttered. "This isn't how I would have wanted you to find out."

"I get the impression you wouldn't have wanted me to find out at all," he spat, his gaze hard as he shot her a look. "And I do struggle with that."

She nodded. "I guess I was trying to avoid unnecessary pain. She did whatever she did, with whoever she wanted, with however many people she had in her life. I was thinking that, if we could just stop the painful disclosures, then she wouldn't still be hurting more people."

"And yet, until it all comes out, no way to know how far that pain will extend."

"That's what we're up against now," she noted, "but, for

the record, I am sorry. If I had found a way to tell you earlier, maybe it would have been easier for you, than to find out now."

He shrugged as he drove along the highway, trying to stay several cars behind Langdon and Roy. "Maybe, yet I'm not sure there's any right way you could ever tell somebody that kind of news," he acknowledged. "So, if you're worried that I'm still blaming you, I'm not. I was just shocked and angry that she would even do that." He took a deep breath and then went on. "As I had a chance to really think about it, I realized how much pain you were already going through, and still are, so why don't we just call it even?"

She gave him a brilliant smile that startled him with the power behind it. She nodded. "I would really like to do that."

He grinned, feeling better than he thought possible. "It seems as if we've been on the outs for a very long time," he admitted. "I guess that's probably what it was, wasn't it, at least in part?"

"That's a lot of it," she said, with a smile. "I was withholding something from you, and I didn't know how to tell you. Yet, in your heart of hearts, you also knew that something was off, but you didn't know what it was, and it was much easier not to look."

"Maybe," he conceded. "I'll do some self-analyzing on all those issues later, much later."

She burst out laughing. "Got it," she replied, still grinning. "Believe me ... I did a bunch of that myself."

"Why?" he asked, shooting her a look. "You're not the one who betrayed your fiancé and your sister."

"True, but if you think she did it without spewing a bunch of poison when she got caught, you're wrong. And some of that poison made me stop and do some soul-searching. Was I really that horrible person she accused me of being?" She stopped and took a deep breath. "It's not easy at any time, but, when it's family, you have to stop and ask yourself whether it was just nastiness on her part or was there more behind it?"

"Poison on her part," Riff stated instantly. "Whatever was going on with her, it apparently had the power to turn her into somebody I didn't recognize. Then again, I wonder if I would have recognized it in her if she wasn't using energy as a screen."

"Meaning?"

"Did she use energy as a way to make our relationship happen in the first place?" he asked. "And was it the energy that made her the person I understood her to be? Not suspecting anything, did I even know the truth about her from the start, or was it all just some subterfuge she used from the get-go?"

"I have to admit I wondered that myself," Angela replied, "because the two of you were a bit of a mismatch."

When he frowned at her, she shrugged. "I mean, you were never home, and she was very much an out-on-the-town gal who liked to go on trips and to go on dates in the evenings. But you were never there, and she didn't seem to care, which for me was very odd. Now I know she didn't care because she was preoccupied with other people's partners," she noted, staring out the window, then groaned. "I try to work my way through this, think it's all good, then something hits me, and I realize I haven't quite let it go," she shared, twisting in her seat to look at him. "I mean, you do what you can do, until something triggers a response, and you realize that you've still got shit to deal with."

He nodded. "And probably will for a while," he said cheerfully.

"*Great*, thanks for that," she quipped, with an eye roll. "Still, this is nowhere near as toxic, as strong, or as emotionally impactful as it was back then, so obviously I am getting somewhere."

"And that *getting somewhere* is huge."

During the rest of the drive back to the hotel, they ended up sharing small talk, little bits of conversations here and there, almost as if getting to know each other again, especially after so much anger and resentment had been between them.

When he pulled up to the hotel, he looked at her intently. "Not sure we've ever just talked like this before."

"I don't think so," she said. "As I look back, my sister was constantly in between us all the time."

He nodded. "I didn't even really get to meet you until we'd been going out for a few months already."

"I know, and I did ask her about you a couple times, but she would never tell me anything."

As he hopped out, he walked around to the back, pulled out some boxes, and asked, "Was there a reason for that?"

"I don't know." Angela shrugged. "She'd had a bunch of boyfriends between your dates," she noted, with an apologetic look in his way. "She always seemed to have somebody else."

He nodded. "That's true. Even when I first met her, she was already going out with somebody," he noted, as he thought about it. "Yet I can't remember who it was."

"I'm pretty sure it was the same guy she ended up going back to all the time," she stated bitterly.

He turned to her. "Seriously? Johnny Waco? The guy

who was killed with her at the motel?"

She nodded. "I don't have any way to verify that, but I'm hoping her diaries will tell me how long this has been going on with her and Johnny Waco. Yet I definitely got the impression that the relationship between them was something she both loved and hated."

"Jesus," Riff swore under his breath. "That is something we definitely should know, if that's the case." He stopped at the thought, then shook his head.

Angela added, "It also wouldn't be cool if it was a love-hate relationship because that means she could have been involved in all kinds of his criminal activities. And, more than that, anybody who knew about their relationship would assume she knew something, and maybe he had gotten her involved to the point that she became a target as well."

"So, that means it might not have been an accident that she was at the motel and killed at the same time as Johnny Waco," he pointed out, staring at her.

"So an attack on both of them was the plan all along."

"Great, so now we have even more suspects."

"But first we need to know how far back her relationship with Waco went."

He looked at her and nodded. "Why are you thinking it went that far back?"

"One of her friends—Tamara, who I talked to—she mentioned something about Sadie's relationship with Waco being off and on for a long time, which could be explained by his various times in jail. And I do remember hearing Sadie herself talk about somebody she knew wasn't good for her but was kind of like a drug. Then she would laugh and say something about how any drug is all about control. I'm not sure if she meant that he was somebody she could control or that her reaction to him was something she couldn't control."

Riff shook his head at that. "The thing about drugs is they get in under your skin and dominate all your waking thoughts. So I'm guessing she probably thought she could see him whenever she wanted to see him, then keep him out of her life the rest of the time—like she did with me. However, it sounds as if maybe it didn't work out that way with this particular guy."

"Right, and I suspect she also kept him away from me so I wouldn't know."

"Which would also make sense if you would be in a position where you ..." He stopped suddenly.

"What?" she asked.

He sighed, looked at her, and continued. "Where you would judge her for it."

She shrugged. "I probably would have. Early on, if he was a druggie type, I wouldn't have approved. Then later, if she was engaged to you, but was screwing around with mine, what did she need somebody else for?" she asked, almost in a mocking tone. "I don't think she was ever happy with any of them."

"No, and presumably you're including me in that."

She winced. "Yeah, I am. I'm wondering if all of you, men in general, weren't also her way of trying to break free from this addicting guy. Or maybe she held off from seeing him for as long as she could. Then, when she realized she wouldn't have that traditional, normal family life with kids, she was like, *Screw it. I might as well just have fun then.*"

He nodded. "That really would make more sense, particularly if she was trying to break up with him after this long off-and-on-again term. Maybe she just gave up that idea and didn't fight that relationship at that point."

"And that's how she ended up dead," Angela added, "so …"

Riff interjected, "We also know that sometimes these energy-working abilities can completely change someone and sometimes … it could work both ways. Used to benefit others, that energy will benefit the user. However, used to harm others, then that energy can rebound, and that negativity will hit back at the user …"

CHAPTER 10

INSIDE THE HOTEL room, Angela looked up as Royce and Langdon came in. "What happened to you guys? I thought you were ahead of us?"

Langdon smiled. "We were, but we stopped and picked up some food." At the word *food*, her stomach started to growl. "Yeah, ours were growling all the way back here," he noted, with a smile. "It's not exactly the food we would choose, given a better scenario, but it's grub."

And, by then, she smelled the pizza and laughed. "I can't remember the last time I had pizza."

"What?" Riff asked in shock. "It's a critical food group, you know?"

"It so isn't," she argued, with a headshake, yet appreciating his humor.

Langdon looked over at the stack of boxes and sobered a bit. "Did you find anything else?"

"It's triggering some memories for me," she admitted, as she pointed out some of the boxes. "Not so much is there that we particularly need, but definitely some interesting journal entries are there. Then memories came up because some of the entries trigger other things for me. Some that I recognized from her past."

She shrugged and added, "It's obvious that the relationship with Johnny Waco, the guy who died with her, went on a lot longer than we had initially suspected. And that's the thing that triggered something else for me from a long time ago. You know how one thing leads to another and all?"

She explained about her sister's comment on drugs, and their current hypothesis that maybe—when she realized she couldn't have children and that whole normal life—she decided to just stop fighting the attraction to Waco. "Presumably she would have broken up with Riff fairly soon at that point in time."

Riff nodded. "I would think so, but we have no way of knowing where she was mentally at by then," he noted. "I'm willing to give her the benefit of the doubt."

Royce snorted. "You can try to put normal, rational, logical motivations on somebody like that, but it just doesn't always work." Royce took a step to the side table with the pizza on it. "Everybody, come grab some pizza, and then I suggest we call it a night and start fresh in the morning."

Langdon asked, "Does anybody have any other information? It just seems as if the days are running by, and we're not getting anywhere."

"We're doing okay," Riff said. "If you think about it, we've come quite a long way, considering where we started."

"Yet it doesn't seem like it," Angela muttered, as she grabbed a piece of pizza and sat back down again. "It feels as if we're close to something, but I'm afraid it'll end up the same damn way as before. *Close but no cigar.*"

"Let's not go in that direction. We know an awful lot more this time around, so hopefully we can get this cleared up quickly," Royce stated, with a gentle smile, as he looked over at Riff. "We still have no information on the vehicle used in the drive-by. Or on Chip."

Riff stared back at him. "Right, so we have a shooter out

there, who may or may not have followed us to the storage unit, may or may not have followed us back here again, which means we must watch our backs at every second, at every turn."

"Always," Langdon confirmed.

"That's just a given when we're into these scenarios," Royce added, "but what we really need is to catch a break on who still gives a damn now. Everybody's dead, so why do they even care? What happened to shake all this up after five years?"

"Yeah, it's been five years, but not everybody's dead," Angela pointed out. "Whoever is doing this isn't dead and could be tied into it, one way or another. If he's not our serial killer, maybe he was the third party to Sadie's and Johnny Waco's tryst at the seedy motel? Maybe we should go back to the motel and knock on doors, looking for this Chip person."

Riff grimaced. "We need more than that. We need to link him to Sadie and/or Johnny. So knocking on doors is a good start. At least check in with the motel owner about Chip, if that's not been done yet."

Angela sighed. "I'm really hoping that we won't end up in a big mess. So, what about other known associates?" she asked so suddenly that everyone frowned at her.

Royce stopped midbite. "Did anyone find anything out about that yet?"

Langdon took a bite, then turned to them and shook his head. "None that we've heard yet, but Terk and Jonas are on it, and will let us know if anything comes up."

"Right," she muttered. "That's the next big problem, isn't it?" Everyone went back to eating, and she did as well.

Langdon noted, "It's one thing to think about who the

known associates are, but getting them to talk will be a hardship."

"I get that," she said, "but I think that takes us back to this Chip guy. James was killed for sharing that info with us, as well as the seedy motel. We can't jump to conclusions because we don't know the whole story. Still, chances are, whoever killed James is linked to the one following us." She turned to Langdon and Royce. "Given all that, are you guys staying close by?"

Langdon and Royce both nodded. "Yes, we'll be setting up watches all night," Royce shared, and Langdon nodded in agreement.

She winced. "I won't be much help in that area."

They laughed. Riff added, "Weren't expecting you to be. You need to get some sleep, so you'll be ready for whatever tomorrow brings."

"What's tomorrow?" she asked, turning to look at him. "Outside of the fact that I need to read more of my sister's journals, what are we doing?"

"That depends on you. Read as much and as fast as you can, so we can get answers as quickly as possible. What you've already found has been quite valuable, so the question is, what else is in Sadie's diaries?"

Angela nodded. "In that case, I'll resume my reading." With that, she got up, grabbed the current journal she had started on, and headed to her bedroom. She was a reader, an avid one, but she wasn't looking forward to this particular selection tonight. However, Riff and the guys were right. It was better that she read it than anybody else.

Once she was settled in bed, now thankful for the pizza, she opened up the latest journal and continued to read.

THE NEXT MORNING Riff sat in the kitchenette area, waiting for the coffee to arrive from room service. He'd wanted to make a trip to get it but didn't want to wake anybody. Since everyone would need coffee this morning, this was the best answer.

Angela stumbled out of her bedroom and sat down at the small table beside him. She looked up at him, bleary-eyed.

"You don't look as if you got much sleep," he noted.

She shook her head. "Nothing good about what I was reading last night," she muttered. "Stuff of nightmares, not dreams."

He winced at that. "Sorry, but it did seem as if you were the best person for the job."

"Yeah, I was," she agreed, "but I didn't really need to know all that about my sister."

He stared at her for a moment. "I'm sorry for that too. It has to be hard. I almost hate to ask, but did you find anything pertaining to the case?"

"Possibly," she replied, "but I'm not sure. I can confirm that she had a long-term relationship with Johnny Waco, way before you were ever in the picture, but she also broke it off years ago, from what I could tell. Then he reappeared, probably freshly released from prison, and they struck up a relationship again, and that's when she started getting in trouble. She admitted that he found her when she was at a low point in her life, and all her arguments about not starting another affair with him just seemed to go out the window. Then, once she'd started the charade, she couldn't stop."

He nodded slowly. "Which gels with what we already knew."

"Sure," she agreed, "but it still sucks."

"It does," he murmured. "Nothing nice about finding out things you don't like or even want to know in regard to your family, … but we aren't here to judge her. We're only here to find out what happened to her."

Angela gave him a wide smile. "Yeah, I hear that, and I understand it, but it still sucks that I have to scrape through her personal life to sort out what happened to her," she murmured. "I would prefer to skip this step."

He looked at her intently. "Did you finish?"

She nodded. "I figured it would be a whole lot easier to just get through it all, and then maybe I could have a day without all that running through my head." Then she yawned and looked up at him hopefully. "Any chance of coffee? I'm feeling pretty trashed right now."

"I've got coffee coming. The guys are getting some sleep. Royce and Langdon took watches, despite the fact that I was wide awake."

She nodded and looked around the suite. "I guess they probably took the rooms beside us then?"

"Yes, thankfully it's the easiest answer. They've been running back-and-forth all night, keeping watch," he shared, "but it's been quiet."

"Of course it's been quiet," she muttered, followed by another yawn. "Do we really think someone cares?"

"Someone shot at us. So, yes, someone cares. Any idea who it was?"

"There was a mention of some unnamed *friend* of Waco's. Somebody who was apparently going places, and Johnny Waco wanted to go along for the ride. But somewhere along the line—whether it was about Sadie or what, I'm not so sure—but whenever, they decided that they might do better on their own."

He winced at that. "That'll never go down well."

"No, and there was some talk … Gimme me a minute, and I'll go grab it. I turned down the corners of every page that mentioned something important, but she didn't use full sentences or full explanations. So a lot of it is little bits and pieces as she tried to sort her way through it at one point. She mentioned something about … Wait." She tried to collect her thoughts, then added, "It was something about looking for a way out, more or less." She shot him a sideways glance. "As if they were both looking for a way out."

"So, for Johnny Waco to get out or for her?"

"I think for both," she replied and shrugged. "In all honesty, I think they were looking to find a life for themselves."

"So that means what? They couldn't just walk away?" he asked.

"I'm guessing he needed a score, some compelling reason to make her go with him. As you very well know, Sadie wasn't one for suffering or for going without or living in poverty or anything along that line," she stated, with a wave of her hand. "I mean, the details don't matter, but … this wasn't very long before her death. So whatever that score was could theoretically be what got them messed up. I just don't know what that was. She doesn't come out and say, *Hey, we'll steal drugs from the local gangs and sell them again* type of thing. It just mentioned that Johnny's got a plan, an idea to get them out of this mess and to find a way to have a life together." She looked over at him and shrugged. "Sorry."

Riff shook his head. "At this point in time, it's beyond *sorry*. Besides, it's not your fault, and it's not my fault either," he added. "This was all Sadie's doing."

Angela nodded. "It would really be good if we could finally accept that," she muttered. "I'm still a long ways off."

He smiled. "You're a whole lot closer than you think."

Ruefully she shook her head. "Then it comes out and hits you again."

"And it's likely to do that for a very long time," he replied, "but we're both okay. We're fine, and whatever she got herself into? ... Maybe, if she had had a chance to rethink it, she may not have gone down that path. Yet it seems she did, and no way we can do anything about it now."

"True that."

He stared at her. "I know I said it already, but I truly feel awful and owe you an apology for the way I've treated you all this time."

She sighed. "Actually I owe you an apology. I mean, not only did I *not* tell you what I knew, I didn't—"

He just shook his head. "How about we just call it a truce?"

"A truce works," she said. "Seems we agreed to that earlier. ... How about we not mention it again." She reached out a hand and was surprised as he shook hers.

"Was that necessary?" he asked, with a note of humor. "The shaking on it, I mean."

"I would give you a hug, but that still seems to be taboo, you know?"

He stared at her. "Since when is a hug taboo?"

She frowned at him. "Since your body language has been telling me to stay away forever."

He wrinkled up his face, raising his hands in surrender. "Obviously I've got some shit to work my way through, but, for the record, a hug is something I would never be against," he shared. "I did find a lack of physical contact sometimes in my relationship with your sister. I'm not talking about sex. I mean, physical touch in general. As if hugs were something she never seemed to want."

Angela frowned at him. "That should have told you something."

"It probably did," he admitted, "and I just didn't want to listen."

"I get that," she replied. "The good part is that you get to consider what you want in a relationship now."

"Yeah, *when* I'm done with all this," he said, as he eyed her closely. "What about you? What will you do when this is over?"

"Same as I'm doing now. Maybe I'll sign up to do some work with the lovely healer ladies back home and see if I can learn more about energy-based healing and help my patients in a bigger, better way. Terkel said that we can talk about it, and that sounds good enough for now."

He smiled. "You've always been about healing, haven't you?"

"Absolutely."

"And what if you find you can't have a family?" he asked curiously.

She smiled. "If I can't, I can't. I'm not sure what I'm supposed to say to that, but, if there was ever a place to get pregnant," she quipped, "it's likely to be at Terk's place."

He stared at her, shocked for a moment, and then he started to laugh and laugh. "Now that is very true. And the healers could quite possibly help too, couldn't they?" He was truly curious more than anything else.

"That would be my understanding, but I wouldn't want to push it."

"No, of course not, but still, that group has some pretty amazing skills."

"Skills and a lot of heart," she noted. "With this many babies around that place, if I wanted to get pregnant, it makes me think that would be the perfect place to do it."

Riff had to chuckle at that. "So, what will you do? Invite a boyfriend over and implement the whole hired-sire philosophy?"

She shook her head. "No, not if I don't have to. I would much prefer to be a family instead of a single parent, but it doesn't always work out that way and—" Just then came a knock on the door, a special knock, and she stopped whatever she was about to say.

He got up, quite relieved to have a change in the conversation, but he couldn't for the life of him say why. As he opened the door, Langdon stood there, pushing a cart inside. "This came for you, and I figured you might want to share it with us."

"Oh, yes." Riff opened the door wide enough to allow for the cart and Langdon and Royce to all enter.

At that, Langdon took one look at her and smiled. "Did you get some sleep?"

"A little, but not exactly good sleep."

"Ah, so does that mean you read the diaries all night?"

She shrugged. "Somebody had to go through it."

"Anything?"

"Nothing more than what I would have expected." Angela explained the little bit that she had found and had already told Riff.

"It makes sense," Langdon replied, with an understanding nod. "All we really need is the name of the person Johnny Waco was working for at the time because it sounds as if a double-cross was going on."

"Maybe," she replied, "but no names were mentioned." She looked back at Riff. "Those messages from James, the prisoner, what did he say again?"

He noted, "That he had something more to tell us, something that he should have told us before but didn't. Of course now we can't ask him anything."

"So, that would most likely be the name of the third party in their tryst or the murderer's name, or the guy Waco worked for and maybe was stealing from. So probably that message ended up getting James killed, even without sharing names," she murmured. "It seems like quite an unlikely coincidence otherwise."

Riff nodded.

"Yeah, that's quite possibly what happened," Angela agreed. "But do you suppose James might have told someone else who could give us answers?" she asked, looking at the guys, who all were deep in thought.

Riff pondered that and then said, "I'll ask Jonas to take a look into that." And with that, he got up and walked off to the side and made his phone call and quickly explained what they were thinking.

"I'll look into it," Jonas replied. "James had just been moved into another area of that prison, so it's possible."

"Why was he moved?" he asked.

"Supposedly to keep him safer, until the move to the new prison came about," Jonas replied in a wry tone, "but apparently we played right into somebody's hands."

"Find out who was involved in that because James clearly got moved closer to his death, so somebody knows something."

"Yeah, yeah, I'm on it, but inmates with intel are dropping like flies. You do realize that prison snitches aren't easy to find, right? Especially if you expect me to have an answer in a couple of days. So, you guys got anything new?" After hearing what they had found in the locker, Jonas whistled. "That just makes this even more your kind of case, you know? That's the kind of woo-woo shit that nobody here can even begin to deal with."

"So you say," Riff replied, with a smile. "I'm not so sure that you're right though."

"Eventually we'll get to the bottom of it, and then we can try to deal with whatever the fallout is," Jonas shared. "Regardless you know that anything to do with *energy work* isn't something we can take to court."

"We'll see where it leads us. We're still hoping to find some solid answers."

"Let's hope so because nobody else can do it." And, with that, Jonas rang off.

Riff rejoined them and shared, "Jonas will look into it, but he didn't sound terribly enthusiastic or encouraging."

Langdon shrugged. "More to the point, the minute energy work becomes involved, as far as he's concerned, it doesn't have anything to do with him. He is old-school in that way," he mentioned, looking at her.

Angela nodded. "Yet we don't know if my sister was using energy on anyone but us, theoretically keeping us out of the loop. We don't know if she used it on Johnny or for Johnny, or if somebody else in their criminal world knew what she was doing and decided she was too dangerous to live. It's possible she used it against somebody with energy skills themselves, and they weren't happy when they found out." She added, with a shrug, "We won't know unless we can get whoever is behind this to admit it."

"Confessions happen more in the movies than in real life," Riff noted.

She winced. "There goes that whole fantasy world I was hoping for," she admitted, with a chuckle.

CHAPTER 11

ABOUT AN HOUR after they finished breakfast, the four of them were sitting in the hotel suite, trying to figure out what to do next, when Jonas phoned with a list of people the informant, James, had met in jail on that last day of his life.

"Oh good," Riff noted. "We need a rundown on them."

"I already sent their files from the prison to you and to Terk," he added, "but we're not seeing anything so far. Yet Terk and his crew are doing a deep dive. Just don't expect anything to pop today."

"Right, but if anybody there might have cheerfully accepted some money for the job, we could work with that."

"We could hope for that, and Terk mentioned following the money, but still somebody would need to get to James too."

Riff agreed. "Yeah, but we know those bad guys have their ways to do these things."

"Too damn easily if you ask me," Jonas stated, reminding them of the harsh realities of prison life. And, with that, Jonas ended the call again.

"We have a list of names," Riff announced, turning to the others. "I suggest we each take a batch to read and get started, trying to figure out who, where, and what we've got. Let's see if we can come up with any connection between one of these guys and Johnny Waco."

"The problem with that though," Langdon pointed out, "is that a lot of people in prison would have just killed James for money. It would not be personal or otherwise motivated. I mean, somebody with a life sentence doesn't care, and they're not planning on getting out, so they're just trying to make their life easier," he explained. "So, you could include everyone with a life sentence on that reasoning alone. Plus, you know that Terk and his team are on it, and, with their computers, they will find anything faster than we can by doing a manual search."

"Agreed. If not the inmates, other suggestions then?" Riff asked, staring at him. "We need to talk to all of Waco's known associates. We don't have any DNA on this third guy involved in their tryst. We don't have anything."

Angela shook her head. "We don't know the ID on the third DNA," she clarified. "I mean, obviously we know the DNA came from the bed where three people left behind blood that night," she noted, carefully avoiding the use of her sister's name. "What we don't know is whether any other forensic information has been found."

"That will take a bit of time too," Langdon warned her. "Jonas might get a rush on it, but it'll still take time to process. We also don't have any tox screens or similar types of evidence to help tell us what went on. Too much time has passed for most forensic evidence as well."

Riff nodded, then turned to Angela and asked, "You're sure there's nothing in the diaries?"

She frowned. "I was pretty tired when I got to some of the later entries," she admitted. "I guess I can go back over them again."

"Again, and then possibly again," Royce suggested. "I

know it's got to be painful, but, if there is even the slightest mention of a hint of another person, we need to know it."

She nodded, then got up, grabbed the last diary in the time line, and sat off to the side.

"If you want one of us to help," Royce added, "I'm willing to give you a hand."

"In a way, you would be better off, just because I get sucked into it with all the emotional stuff." She handed him three of the diaries. "Knock yourself out."

He groaned as he looked down at them. "Please tell me it's not full of fantasies or stuff like that."

She burst out laughing. "No, nothing like that. It's all about the mess of her life and how she couldn't have children. Fantasies might be easier."

He winced and nodded. "Fine, you owe me then."

"Hey, you volunteered," she reminded him, with spirit. He laughed and agreed. By the time she'd gone through some of the other diaries again, she had one more in front of her, and honestly it was the one she'd been avoiding. It was probably the one she should have gone through first, but it was just so damn hard to read her sister's thoughts in all this. Even though it had been five years, it had a way of making it seem like just five minutes ago.

She looked over at Royce first, before beginning a reread of this last journal. "Find anything?"

He shook his head. "Nothing. It's frustrating that there would be this much information and yet nothing useful." He looked at the last diary installment and raised his eyebrows. "You or me?"

She winced. "How about you?"

But just then his phone rang, so she grabbed the final diary in the meantime and started on it. She hadn't gone very far when she noted the mention of a pawn shop. Not so much a name but a location. She frowned as she kept going, flipping through the pages. When she looked up, Riff stared at her.

"What's wrong, Angela?"

"Sadie talks about a particular pawn shop that Johnny used to go to all the time. Sounds as if they were relatively professional, yet not so much. Like a regular pawn shop on the inside, but they did dirtier deals in the back."

He nodded. "That's not exactly a strange thing. A lot of those industries do have backroom deals just like that."

"Well, this guy's got a connection to the pawn shop."

He walked over, his gaze sharp. "What kind of a connection?"

She pointed out the passage. "Maybe you should take a look."

He sat down and read it out loud. "*If it wasn't for the idiot at the pawn shop, we would be doing much better.*" He frowned at her.

She shrugged. "I don't know what that means."

He nodded and kept reading, but this time to himself. When he stopped a few minutes later, he tapped the book and showed her the mention of the pawn shop. "She does mention a name, but it's an odd one." He looked over at the rest of the team. "What pawn shop has *Mormon* in the name?" He stared at them, waiting for a reply.

Royce snapped his fingers. "There is one. It doesn't have the greatest reputation. Seems it changed hands a while back, when the parents passed or something. If it's the one I'm thinking about, it could be a possibility," he murmured.

"Get us a rundown on everybody there." Riff looked over at her and smiled. "You know, this just might have been useful after all."

She nodded, then grimaced at the diary in his hand. "Why didn't I see that last night?"

"Because you weren't thinking of a pawn shop or any physical place. You were thinking in terms of the name of a person to help us, something that would be a whole lot more specific," he said. "This could be the break we're looking for." Riff handed Royce the diary. "Fresh eyes," Riff said, as Royce snatched it up. "Particularly if you see anything about a pawn shop."

Royce turned the pages and read through a bit. "There was something about a business, and there was a *Mormon* mention." He flipped through this edition and pointed out the passage that he had seen and handed it over.

Riff read it again. "Yes, this is it. Something else is here, a mention of a big score too."

"Yeah, but what's the big score? Scoring off whom?" Angela asked in exasperation.

Riff shrugged. "Sounds like neither Johnny nor Sadie had any money to take off and leave. She either needed a rich guy to take her along or she needed to steal some. Besides, you mentioned Sadie writing how she needed a score before."

"Right." She searched her memory and nodded. "Johnny wanted out, but they needed a big score." She looked at Riff. "When you left on missions, did you leave her any money?"

"No," he replied, puzzled. "Why would I? She was working and lived at my house, where everything was on autopay, whether I was on a mission or not."

"Did you ever pay any of her bills?"

He shook his head. "No, she told me that she was self-sufficient, so I never gave it a thought." She stared at him, and he looked at her and groaned. "She wasn't, was she?"

Angela shook her head. "Sadie lost her job. Not *lost* but she walked away from her job, saying she needed to do something else. I assumed you were helping her out financially."

"She wasn't working at the same job anymore?" he asked, staring at her in shock. "When did that happen?"

"Somewhere around the same time that she started going out with Johnny again."

"Did she … did she quit or was she fired?"

"I don't know, but I do know the owner."

He stared at her, and she nodded, then pulled out her phone. "I guess that's where I'll start."

"Sounds good to me." Riff looked down at the information in the diary. "Why the hell didn't she tell me anything?"

Langdon said the quiet part out loud. "Because you weren't part of her life." When Riff stared at him in shock, Langdon shrugged. "For whatever reason, she'd already written you off." Langon spoke quickly, so as to soften the blow. "She just didn't bother telling you."

At that, Riff swore out loud and long.

Langdon nodded. "Look. I get it, and it sucks, man. I mean, she treated you in a rough way, but we're getting to the bottom of it now, and you know that you're better off knowing the truth, as we all are learning it together now."

Riff nodded and didn't say anything more. Needing to redirect his attention, he focused on Angela, who was off the phone now.

She walked over to him and sat down with a *thump*, looking defeated. "So, I was able to talk to her boss," she began, gaining the attention of all three men. "She worked at a small bookkeeping firm as the receptionist out front." She hesitated and then added, "He didn't want to say anything because she's dead and gone, but, when I explained that we had a fresh lead on her murder and that we were desperately trying to piece some things together, he did admit that she was fired." Sadly she looked at Riff and almost apologetically added, "For stealing."

He stared at her in shock, then slowly shook his head. "Stealing? Good God, I didn't know her at all, did I?"

Angela winced. "She was my sister, and I didn't know her. She didn't say anything to me about it either."

"But, if she was working, why would she need to steal?" he asked. "If she'd gotten in a bind with credit card debt or whatever, I could have helped her."

"Odds are it was more sordid than that," Langdon suggested softly, "so she wouldn't have asked either of you."

Angela nodded. "I don't know what led up to it, but something did, and she got fired. And, without that means of income, she then had no way to pay for gas, for clothes, for whatever else she wanted. She should have had savings," she muttered. "She'd worked at that firm for quite a few years. I know that she spent a fair bit of her paycheck. Yet she was always saving for that rainy day, so she should have been okay."

"But that's assuming she's the girl she was before, the one you thought she was. Either way, she would also have seen that rainy day was coming a whole lot faster and probably didn't like where it would take her," Langdon pointed out. "A rainy day is one thing, but, when you see a whole host of rainy days and realize you need to get another job, maybe in her frame of mind at the time, she just didn't want to, which kind of explains her overall behavior."

Angela nodded. "I think by that time, she was going through this whole personality crisis, so a new job was not likely on her radar. I'm not making excuses for my sister, and it would be nice if I could understand the choices she made and the people she hurt in the meantime. However, she didn't share any of that in these diaries. ... It seems as if these are just painful meanderings of ... I don't want to say a mind going around the bend, but some churning is evident here." She looked over at Royce. "What did you get out of them?"

"A mind going around the bend," he agreed, then shrugged. "No, not quite, but she was going through a personal crisis of some sort. That much is obvious."

She nodded. "That I would agree with, and I think we're just seeing the outer limits of whatever decisions she made at that time."

Langdon popped up, staring at his phone, and interjected, "So, the pawn shop is still there. According to the police file I've got here, it's had multiple infractions and has been fined several times, but they've never been able to prove anything serious. However, it's a well-known hotspot for moving stolen goods. Yet every time the cops go in there, they can't find anything to really crack down on. So, it's under watch, but it's never really been taken down."

"Which means we need to go pay them a visit," Angela stated. At that, Riff turned and glared at her. She just shook her head. "No, we really do, and I need to go along."

"And why is that?" Riff asked.

"Because I still look like my sister," she stated, "and, if there is one thing we need, it's for them to talk to me. And, if that breaks the ice a little bit, I'm okay with it."

The others looked over at Riff, and he nodded slowly.

"I'm not okay with it, but it probably is a good idea."

"One problem," she noted, "is that we have no idea what kind of relationship she had with the owner."

Riff groaned and asked the others, "Are we all going?"

"Yes," Langdon replied, as he stood up. "This could easily be our shooter," he pointed out in exasperation. "Let's not send one team in and leave the other one sitting here doing research. Better still, we all go in with a show of force, so they don't think you're alone. Then let's see what we can figure out."

Riff suggested, "I'll go in with Angela. I think you two should be nearby, watching foot and vehicle traffic."

And that's what they did.

She wasn't anywhere near as cocky as she hoped to be as she sat in the vehicle outside the pawnshop. She looked over at Riff, who was staring at her.

"You don't have to go in, you know?"

"Yet it feels as if I do," she muttered. "It just feels as if my sister needed help, and I wasn't there for her."

He nodded. "If you feel like that, then let me put your mind at ease. I'm not sure she would have accepted any help from you anyway."

"No, she wouldn't have," she agreed, "but I still need to do this." And, with that, she hopped out. He got out with her, and together they walked up to the front entrance of the pawnshop. In a conversational tone, she added, "I don't think I've ever been in a pawn shop before."

"In some cases, they can be a good place to get most anything you need secondhand," he shared, "but sometimes items are stolen goods. Thus you could be buying something that somebody cried a lot of tears over when giving it up. So, it all depends on what kind of people you want to deal with."

"I hadn't considered that," she said. "So, I guess a lot of people who come here are desperate, aren't they?"

"They're looking for money, and generally that's because times are tough," he explained, as he pulled open the door, and they stepped inside.

Immediately a younger male stepped out from the back room and frowned at them. "Can I help you?"

"Yes," she replied, with a gentle smile.

"What are you looking for?" he asked, as he walked closer.

"Information."

He stiffened at the single word and shook his head vehemently. "Absolutely not. No way. I don't deal in information."

"I wasn't thinking you were dealing in it," she clarified carefully. "However, my sister was murdered, and we've found a reference to somebody at this place. I just need five minutes of your time."

He stared at her in shock. "What the hell are you talking about? I'm the only one here, and it's my business."

She studied him, then added, "Were you the owner around five years ago?"

His expression cleared, and he nodded, giving a sigh of relief. "I did buy the business from my family, but I'm sure any research would tell you that, before we had the sale closed, they were killed in a car accident."

She stared at him. "I'm so sorry. That must have been terrible."

"Since I was buying the business, it was very fortuitous." He smirked. "But the old man was a good guy," he added soberly. "He is sorely missed."

She nodded, not sure what to think of anybody who

would consider the death of their parents as *fortuitous*, but maybe all that meant was that he didn't have to pay for the business. So good luck for him. "Did you keep the business the same as before?"

He nodded. "Pretty much. I expanded, opened a few borders," he stated proudly. "Other than that, it's mostly the same. Why kill off something that works? Right?"

"Oh, that's a good way to look at it," she agreed.

"Now, what were you talking about again? Some chick who got murdered?" he asked, eyeing Riff at her side. "I don't know anything about that."

"It's in the diary that we have. She talks about Johnny, who was murdered as well."

He frowned at her. "Johnny? I thought you said it was a girl."

Angela nodded. "My sister. Her name was Sadie."

He shrugged. "So, what's the deal with this Johnny guy?"

"Johnny Waco was her lover. We've recently found the real crime scene where she and Waco were killed at the same time and place, with their DNA to prove it."

"So, Johnny killed this chick or what?" he asked, seemingly confused.

"We don't think so," Angela replied. "We found the crime scene of my sister's murder, and ..." She hesitated, stumbling over her words a bit. "Sorry, I'm not trying to ramble, but obviously it's an emotional time for me."

He remained frozen, an odd stillness to his stance. "I'm still confused. What does any of this have to do with me?"

"Johnny was in business with somebody from this pawn-shop," she replied, sounding a bit more collected. At that moment, the room went silent.

RIFF WATCHED THE look in the other man's eyes, going from curious to wary and now a deep anger. Riff stepped forward and murmured, "She's not trying to insult anybody."

The other man was not appeased, and he glared as he replied, "She sure as hell was. I don't know what the hell you think you guys are doing, but you're not cops, and you've got no business talking to me like that. I didn't have anything to do with that."

Whether Riff believed him or not, Riff recognized that they had touched a nerve with this guy and had gone as far as they could go for now. He reached for Angela's arm and tugged her backward. She glared at him, then turned to face the man behind the counter. "It was just a question, so why does that bother you so much?"

"You didn't even ask a question," he snapped. "You're insinuating that I had something to do with murdering a young woman. How is that supposed to not piss me off?"

"I guess it depends on whether you did it or not," she said, with a wave of her hand. "If you didn't, and you're innocent, then who gives a crap? Nothing personal, I'm just trying to find justice for my sister."

"That's a nice thought and all," the guy said, "but, if your sister was hanging out with Johnny Waco, believe me that she was no saint herself."

Angela stiffened at that, but then nodded. "You're right. She was no saint, and there was probably no saving her either, but that doesn't mean she deserved to be murdered and to be dropped off on an overpass, like a piece of garbage."

"She was a piece of garbage if that's the chick I saw him with back then. You must have been the lucky one in the family because she was a nutcase," he muttered.

"When did you ever see her?" she asked, staring at him in shock.

He shrugged. "With Johnny."

"So, you personally knew Johnny?"

He nodded. "Sure, I knew Johnny, back before he went to jail. That guy was always destined to end up in the slammer. He was always bad news, always."

She nodded. "I was hoping that you might know something more."

"No, you were hoping I might have killed her and would casually mention it," he suggested, with a snort. "So you're as whacked out as she was?"

Angela stiffened, then relaxed. "It wasn't like that. I'm just trying to find answers as to who might have killed my sister."

"I get that. Believe me that I understand those things, but I didn't have anything to do with it."

"Good," she said, surprising him. Even Riff wondered where she was going. She gave the guy a bright smile and then casually asked, "In that case, do you know who would?"

He stared at her for a good ten seconds and retorted, "Look, chickee …"

She winced. "Please, call me anything but that."

He glared at her. "As I was saying, I don't know anything about it."

"But you obviously thought that Johnny was a loser and that she was too."

"Yeah, she had a death wish, and that's the closest I can say to figuring it out. Once she started into drugs with him, it was a one-way street."

"Did you ever see her taking drugs?" she asked curiously because, in her mind, Sadie never had used drugs. She never saw it anyway.

"She took light stuff," he said, with a shrug. "I did see her smoking a joint occasionally. Usually it was outside, while I was talking to Johnny."

"Did Johnny ever bring you stolen goods?"

He stared at her. "You really know how to kill a conversation."

She groaned. "It would be really nice if people would just give us the damn information we need so we can solve her murder and be on our way."

"I don't know anything about her damn murder," he muttered. "And I really don't like you being here. You're bad for business."

She looked around the completely empty store and the equally empty parking lot behind the store, raising an eyebrow. He glared at her in return. "Hey, I just want information to help me find out what happened to my sister. Give me something, some other path to follow, and I'll head off and follow it."

He groaned. "You won't quit, will you?"

"No, I won't. I can't."

At that, he narrowed his gaze and studied her. "Guilt is a horrible reason for finding answers."

Angela sighed. This guy behind the counter might look like a loser, but he was seasoned and could fling arrows himself. "Sometimes that's all you've got," she murmured, staring at him, "and I get it. You've probably lived an entirely blameless life. But, for me, my sister was important, and I don't like the way it ended between us."

"Toward the end she was getting pretty wild," he admitted. "Crazy wild."

She nodded. "I don't know so much about that part of it. We had quite a row not too long before."

"Maybe that's what set her off then. What was the fight about?"

She shrugged. "She was screwing my fiancé."

He stared at her and then laughed. "Doesn't that beat all?"

"No, not really, not if she was on that same self-destructive path you were talking about. In fact, it kind of makes more sense."

"I don't know where her head was at. She always acted as if she was superior, a know-it-all," he shared. "I can't stand that in a woman. At the end of the day, she didn't look all that great. I don't know where she was at mentally, but it wasn't sane. It wasn't normal. All I can say is that she was going through some stuff."

"Yeah, she was going through some stuff, but I'm not sure that the stuff she was going through was necessarily anything traumatic."

"I don't know either, but she got louder. She got noisier. She drank more, and, whenever she was around Johnny, … she was hanging on to him as if he was the answer to all her problems. Little did she know that he wasn't an answer for anybody. Meanwhile, when acting that way, she was stroking his ego pretty good." The guy snorted.

"Yeah?"

"He started bringing in some shit, but it was mostly bad-news stuff, and I couldn't deal with it," the guy shared. "I tried to keep the business legit. Now my dad? … Well, he had a couple sidelines going that were not so legit, but I've worked hard to keep it clean since I took over."

Riff looked around, his gaze focused a little more carefully as he listened to what this guy was saying. He wasn't sure whether he believed him or not, though it was coming across as being quite possible, yet it still wasn't necessarily the truth. "Does anybody else work for you here?" Riff asked. He swiveled back to study the owner's reaction, but it was a quick headshake, followed by a simple response.

"No, it's just me. I don't make that much money, but, if it's just me, I do okay. And believe me, once you start hiring staff, you end up with trouble," he said. "Everybody wants a cut of the pie, or they think they need a raise, or they want to take shit home that they want from the store—without paying for it. It's usually the better stuff that I'll make money on, and they want it at a prime price or just for free," he muttered. "So, no, I prefer to work alone."

She nodded, and Riff was surprised that she kept persisting, wanting more info.

Even the owner was getting irritated. "Look, lady. You're starting to piss me off. I've got a business to run, so you need to go. I gave you five minutes, and now you just won't lay off."

"That's because I'm looking for something I can take with me," she cried out in frustration.

He leaned over the counter, glaring at her. "I don't have anything for you."

"Did Johnny hang out with anybody else?" Riff asked. "Did he have a partner? Somebody who did jobs with him?"

The owner now glared at him. "And, if he did, then what?"

"Then we want to talk to him."

"Why? I mean, if you only found their DNA, the two of

them at the motel, that should have been enough. Johnny probably killed her himself and got away with it. Then he went on and finally got picked up for some other piece of shit job because he was like that, and now you're just too late to make him pay."

"Maybe," she replied, but she took a deep breath, unsure how much she wanted to relay this news, but still thought it was worth a try. "There was DNA to prove a third person was there."

At that, he stiffened, then turned to her.

She nodded. "See? So I really need to know if Johnny Waco hung out with anybody else."

He pondered that for a moment. "Johnny did have a buddy that he did a bunch of jobs with. And that guy did not like your sister at all."

"Any idea why?"

He laughed. "Nobody needed a why. Your sister was a loose cannon. She seemed completely normal, sweet as could be, but then something weird would happen, and she would change completely. I did talk to Johnny about it once, and he told me that she might have been a loose cannon, but he still really cared about her. I told him that he should find somebody who was a whole lot less work, and he agreed."

"So why wouldn't Johnny get rid of her?"

"I don't know, but he mentioned that she had abilities that he couldn't find elsewhere."

At that, Riff stiffened. "Did he say what abilities?"

The owner gave him a dry look. "No, but I assumed it was, you know, bedroom abilities. Why else would you stay with someone that crazy?"

"She was never erratic before," Angela pointed out, staring at him intently.

"Maybe not, but, when she was around here, she was getting worse. She went from being not friendly to standoffish and superior, then started demanding better prices, more money, and asking what kind of stuff I wanted, as if they would go out and get it for me," he shared, with a headshake. "She was changing, and I didn't like it. I don't like unstable to begin with, but, in this case, it was odd *and* unstable."

"Damn," she muttered.

"Yeah, sorry. When it's your sister, that sucks," he said, "but I'm not surprised she ended up where she did because she sure as hell was starting to ask for it." And, with that, he pointed at the door and stated, "Now it's time for you to go. I've got work to do." He walked over to the front door and held it open for them, giving them no other option but to walk outside.

She glared at him but then walked out. Riff was a little slower, letting her cool off a bit. As he stepped outside, he looked at the owner intently. "Did you ever have any suspicion that Sadie was into anything else?"

He nodded. "I'm not telling her that," he said, pointing at Angela, "but Sadie was into some weird esoteric stuff. I didn't even bring it up because it gives me the heebie-jeebies. But something weird was about that chick. … Like, if you told me that she was a witch, I wouldn't have a problem believing it, and I think she put a spell on Johnny."

"And the other guy, the one he worked with?"

He shrugged. "Not sure I want to tell you his name because what if he didn't have anything to do with it, you know?"

"Then he wouldn't care," Riff replied smoothly.

He groaned. "His name is Chip, but he was just a

flunky. That's all I've got for you. Before you ask me about it, no, I don't know where the hell he is. I haven't seen him since forever."

"Good enough," Riff said. "We'll roust him out."

"Yeah? How will you do that? The guy is probably long gone in the wind."

"Maybe," Riff conceded, "but, when it comes to shit like this, sometimes people have very long memories." And, with that, he followed Angela back out to the parking lot.

Just as the front door went to slam behind him, the pawn shop owner yelled, "Watch out. Chip's weird."

"Weird in what way?" Riff asked, turning.

"As in crazy weird, as in that cultish woo-woo thing again. The two of them could be a hell of a pair, but she was with Johnny, though I'm not sure that wasn't part of the problem." And, with that, he headed back inside and out of view, slamming the door shut.

CHAPTER 12

ANGELA HOPPED UP into the truck, and, when Riff was inside with his door shut, she asked, "Did the pawn shop owner tell you something interesting?"

He nodded. "Yeah, Chip was the name of the guy Johnny hung around with, a low-level partner-in-crime. The same one our dead inmate mentioned. Yet James mentioned some mobster—definitely *not* low-level stuff. Plus, who told us that Johnny had stolen from someone he shouldn't have?"

"Wasn't that James too?" she asked, yet shrugging.

"We're getting the underlings, but the guy able to kill people in prison is rungs above that. And he'll be hidden from us. He's making sure all links to him die young. Plus, if Sadie tried her forgetting spell on this mob guy, we have to remember Langdon's earlier warning. Some of these bad guys have energy skills themselves. So we need to keep a watch out for him for sure."

"Do you think this pawn shop owner is innocent?"

He shrugged. "He knows the players. Could he have been involved? Yes, maybe. But is that really the case? We would have to prove it," he noted, "and I don't have any way to do so at this point. As for energy, the building is filled with way too many signatures to see clearly."

She groaned. "Do you always have to be so damn proper?" Startled, he looked over at her, and she glared at him.

"You always couch your answers."

"That's because I don't want to jump to conclusions," he explained, narrowing his gaze at her. "That won't get us anywhere."

"Feels as if it'll at least get us somewhere," she muttered.

He grinned. "Nope, it doesn't. However, the owner wasn't alone when we arrived. Somebody slipped into the back room as soon as we opened the door and stepped inside. I think that was probably the reason for the delay in talking to us," he shared, as he quickly turned on the engine and headed out of the parking lot and around the block.

"What are you saying?" she asked, turning to him.

"I'm saying that somebody else was in the back of the pawn shop, and I don't think the guy behind the counter told you much because he was afraid that he would be overheard."

"Oh, now that's interesting," she said. "I didn't pick up on that."

He nodded. "You were a little too busy trying to nail his ass to the wall, just in case he was involved."

She winced and had to admit that Riff was probably right. She'd gone in there expecting a fight, maybe even looking for one, and that wasn't good. "I'm sorry. That makes it pretty tough to get answers, doesn't it?"

He shrugged. "You did pretty well though. He opened up quite a bit more than I expected."

"I wondered if he was opening up more just to avoid implicating himself," she murmured. "Yet I don't have any reason for saying that, only that I didn't like him."

"Didn't like him or didn't like him because he didn't like your sister?"

She winced. "She was getting pretty erratic at the end,

you know?"

He looked over at her and shook his head. "No, I didn't know. I was off on a mission and had been gone for six weeks, remember?"

She nodded. "Yeah, sorry about that. I keep expecting you to have been there, but you weren't."

"Apparently, it's a good thing I wasn't," he stated, his tone sharp. "I know that's not what you want to hear, but I don't know how I would have handled finding out that she had been unfaithful," he muttered. "I don't know how you handled it as well as you did."

"I didn't handle it," she snapped. "Why do you think she and I had such a massive blowout?"

He nodded. "I'm not saying that as a criticism, but I'm not sure I would have been as understanding as you were," he clarified. "For me, loyalty is everything. If you say you'll do something, I expect you to do it because your word is your bond. If you say that you love me, I expect you to mean it. If you tell me that you'll marry me and will be there for me every day, I expect that to be true," he explained. "To think that she already went back on those promises while I was out of the country just blows me away. And I did offer many times to change my assignment so that I could stay home and be there with her, but it's not something she wanted. At least it wasn't something she let me know that she wanted," he corrected, "and apparently that's where the problem was."

A long silence filled the truck.

"The pawn shop owner also shared something about this other character, Chip, being involved in the occult, energy stuff. I'm thinking that's what we're talking about here with Sadie too." He shifted lanes as they headed back to the hotel.

Angela sighed. "Yet everybody has such a weird name for it. I mean, if you were to say *energy work* to people, they would think *occult*, wouldn't they?" She stared out the window, hating that, after all this time, they were still rehashing her sister's last days. "I know it's wrong, and that frustrates me, makes me fed up, but a part of me just wishes everything to do with my sister would just die a natural death and go away." She groaned. "Jesus, I feel like an absolute ass for saying that."

"You've been under a lot of stress emotionally, both from her actions and from her demise," he replied. "So you need to let up on yourself and to not feel so guilty about being human and having normal feelings."

"That seems impossible," she muttered, staring at him.

He shrugged. "You feel betrayed, angry, and upset, but the guilt is normal. As is the … Well, I don't want to say *relief,* but that's what it is. Maybe relief that she's gone, relief that you don't have to deal with her shit anymore, relief that you don't have to confront her, relief that you don't have to see her daily and remember all the crap she did to you. All of that's been wiped out because someone killed her."

"It's her actions I have the trouble with," she stated and then winced again. "God, I sound like such a bitch."

"No," he declared. "You don't. You sound like somebody who's been hurting but is trying hard to find a way through this mess." He shrugged. "That's all I'm trying to do too."

She shook her head. "I don't have the right answers—or any answers for that matter. I keep looking for something, for anything, and it just doesn't seem to be there."

"We have another angle to pursue now. I think that's very valuable. We found the pawn shop owner, and he confirmed Chip was working with Johnny. We don't know what else we'll get, but we'll stay on that pathway, and we'll find a way to whatever else we need," he claimed. "This time we will solve this. No way we won't."

She searched his facial expression hopefully. "Do you really think so?"

He nodded. "I do. I think it's about time for us to put this all to rest. I held Sadie in high esteem, feeling horrified and guilty that I wasn't there for her when she was killed," he shared in a somber tone, "only to find out that she wasn't there for me at any point in time. Believe me that there's plenty of guilt to go around here, but I won't take it on— not now that I have a better idea of what was going on in my absence. The fact that I told her that I would cheerfully change jobs and stay home was a big deal to me. She didn't care about that, but now I realize why—because she was never really there for me to begin with," he admitted, with a shrug. "Whatever her problem was, I have to give her the benefit of the doubt and walk away from this as whole as I can. I just want to find answers and get this solved, once and for all. Beyond that," he added, "I don't think we can ask for much more."

"I would like that too," she agreed, staring at him mistily. "You are saying everything that I want to believe is possible, and I don't … I don't want to hate myself anymore."

"Absolutely not. It seems to me that Sadie was always jealous of you. You can't change that now. All you can do is live the life that you always wanted to live, plus live it in the best way you can, in whatever way you want to do it. It is not wrong to want a life for yourself without her. The fact that her death happened and that you're probably feeling guilty for having wished she would go away or die or God-only-knows what other things you probably wished for," he noted, "that's not part of the deal. That's the guilt part that goes along with any mishap," he stated. "So you just need to park those feelings and let it go."

"How did you know I was thinking all those things at one time or another?" she muttered.

He chuckled. "Because it's normal, and it's human. You were hurting—and rightly so. Keep that in mind too. Hurting people hurt other people."

She winced. "That's a phrase for the ages, isn't it?"

He snorted. "It would be more helpful if you would remember it though."

"Maybe," she muttered. "It's tough enough when so much is going on in the world out there right now. Sadie had abilities. She had all these things that she told me she didn't want to deal with, didn't want anything to do with. Yet here she was using her abilities to camouflage what she was truly doing." Angela shook her head. "That's just unbelievable. Why wouldn't she go to healers to see if something could be done for her medical condition?"

"Maybe she did," Riff replied, glancing at her. "Maybe that's exactly what she did. Did she know anybody? Could she have gone to somebody?"

Angela shrugged. "I don't know. I really don't. She never told me about it, and she sure never mentioned it or anybody in the industry. I wouldn't have known anybody to recommend to her, and I didn't offer to help as I'd never learned to do the healing arts part of energy work," she admitted bitterly.

She continued. "I assumed, probably incorrectly, that she would calm down and would find a way to make peace with it. … Having not looked at my own possibilities of having children, I hadn't really understood what that would look like, whether that was even possible. I've certainly dealt with a lot of women who were traumatized because they couldn't have babies. When they did finally get pregnant—and in some cases carried the baby to full term—it's as if their entire world was suddenly complete."

Angela sighed. "I knew that was something my sister really wanted and hadn't had an opportunity to get that kind of help, but I just thought she would keep trying, and maybe her body would heal. … I don't know that I even gave it that much thought," she added, "because we weren't that close anymore. It's one of those things that you think of in passing, but you try not to think of it too much. Whatever was happening to her could potentially be the same outcome for me, so I wanted to block it out even more."

"Again, all I'm hearing is guilt on your side," Riff pointed out. "So remember that you're allowed to be human."

She groaned and nodded. "Where are we going?" she asked, as she looked around, frowning.

"We're following a vehicle."

"What? Why?" she asked, straightening up and looking at the vehicles ahead of them. She saw several trucks, a couple cars, and what looked to be a lorry a little bit farther ahead. She turned to him and asked, "What vehicle and why?"

"Because the driver pulled out from the back of the pawn shop parking lot not soon after you went outside, as if the person was listening in on our conversation, then made a quick escape," he shared. "As I told you earlier, you didn't notice because you were still so upset over him hating Sadie."

She shook her head. "God, and here you were so aware

of everything going on that you could now follow this guy?"

He shrugged. "I only caught it out of the corner of my eye, but it was the distinctive green of the pickup that drew my attention, and I think it's the one up there." He pointed to one of the three vehicles ahead of them. "Second lane over, three vehicles up."

Almost immediately she spotted it and frowned. "So, we could be on a wild goose chase?"

"We could be," he conceded cheerfully, "but it seemed to be a good idea at the time."

"Hey, anything that seems like a good idea is better than what we've got right now." Just then his phone rang. He put it on Speaker to find Langdon on the other end.

"How did it go?" he asked.

Riff quickly relayed the events of their visit. "We're following a vehicle right now that pulled out just ahead of us from the back of the pawn shop," he shared. "I don't know that it has anything to do with us, but it just seemed like interesting timing."

"How so?"

Riff suggested, "Somebody snuck into the back room of the pawnshop when we arrived, but we were not introduced or in any way told somebody else was there. So, when this vehicle left, I figured it was the person sitting in the back, listening."

"You got the license plate?"

"Part of it. I caught a couple letters. I'm getting a little closer now and will see if we can get the rest for you." It took a little maneuvering, some quick lane changes and a bit of luck, but finally he pulled up behind the truck and read off the numbers.

"Got it," Langdon confirmed. "I'll do a quick search on

this and get back to you." And, with that, he was gone.

Angela frowned at Riff. "Why would somebody at the back of the pawnshop care if we knew they were there?"

"It depends on whether the owner's running an honest business and whether that person hiding in the back knew something or if they were involved in something else and just wanted to avoid detection. There are lots of reasons for avoiding people. We don't know that this truck driver knew your sister or that he already knew Johnny, this Chip, or that he had anything to do with the pawn shop—outside of the fact that right now he could be making a delivery, or maybe he picked up something from the pawnshop that belongs to the other guy and walked out of the store with it. How can we know right now?"

"So, we don't know anything."

"All I'm doing is following my instincts."

"Right, and that guy's energy," she added, twisting to face Riff.

He nodded. "And that guy's energy."

She asked, "What is it exactly in the energy that told you to follow it?" He frowned, not wanting to tell her. "I think it's important that you tell me," she persisted.

"Why? Can you stop bugging me about it?"

"No, but do you see a cord? Do you see something between you and it? Is it only your instincts or are you using your energy skills? What is it?"

"I recognize the energy," he shared. "That's all I can tell you."

"Is it familiar?"

"I don't know. Look. I don't know who, how, or why. I just know it's familiar."

She closed her mouth as she stared at the truck and then

shrugged. "I don't get anything familiar about it at all."

"That's not how you use your energy anyway," he pointed out. "I'm very good at finding things that are lost. If Sadie had gone missing, I would have had no trouble finding her that night I called the cops to look for her. That's partly why I was so adamant about getting to the bottom of this."

"I get that much."

"I mean, physically finding my fiancée murdered in the exact way I knew energetically that she would be found in horrifically affected me," he added. "Still, that doesn't give me a free pass for all the rest of the emotions I've been tormented by. Yet it doesn't give her a pass either. Right now I just know. That energy is familiar."

"Familiar from the overpass?" she asked, straightening and turning to him.

He frowned at her. "I don't know that," he said cautiously. "All I can tell you is it's familiar."

Her breath went out with a *whoosh*. "Okay," she muttered. "That's not helpful."

"It might be helpful if we can figure out who this is and where they're heading," he muttered. "We're a little short on information right now."

She nodded and sat back. "I use energy when I'm with my patients," she stated abruptly.

"Good, you're in the right profession. How do you use it?"

"I use it to read people, to assess states of mind, things like that. Although I don't know that I actually see energy as much as intuit it. My sister was quite gifted but me? Not so much."

"Intuition is also energy," he noted, as he quickly changed lanes to follow the target vehicle.

Even as she watched, the driver of the green truck, as if somehow realizing that he was being followed, quickly changed lanes to the left, then pulled a quick turn and disappeared around the corner. Riff followed suit, and she was still open-mouthed at his instant reactions, turning one block farther down. "Is there any chance that we'll still find him?" she asked, twisting to look all around them, searching for the distinctive green truck with no luck.

"We'll find him," Riff declared, with a wolfish grin. "Remember what I do for living? All I can do is find things."

"You don't necessarily find everything though," she pointed out, turning to look at him. "I get that you found Sadie's body, but you didn't find the crime scene."

"No, I didn't, and I wouldn't have looked for that place anyway. I didn't have anything to track back to that motel," he stated. "Right now is a different story. I know what I saw. I know the connection, and I'm on the truck," he snapped. "Hang on tight. We're getting there."

She clutched the door handle and held on as he changed directions, abruptly taking corners again and again. She had no idea where they were, except that they were still going around what appeared to be the same blocks they had been around before. Then he suddenly pulled up in front of a very large apartment building and parked. She stared up at the multiple stories. "You think he's up there?"

"I know he is," he snapped, as he hopped out and walked around to her side. "I suppose there's no chance of your staying here, is there?"

"Nope," she replied, as she hopped out. "No chance at all." He glared at her, and she glared right back. "We're in this together."

His shoulders slumped as he nodded. "But if you get

hurt, I—"

"If I get hurt, I get hurt," she stated. "I can almost hear my sister telling me to not bother."

When he looked at her sharply, she shrugged. "With all this going on, she seems a little closer."

"Do you think she regrets what she did?"

"I think she probably regrets her end result, but I'm not sure that she had any energy for regret. I think she was on a suicide mission to either kill herself or to not care enough to avoid high-risk behavior," she noted, almost in disgust.

"*Great*, so nice to know I wasn't enough to even make her sufficiently happy to want to live."

"I don't think she loved you," Angela added bluntly.

He sucked in his breath. Then he slammed the elevator button with his fist, using a little more force than necessary, while glaring at her. "You don't pull any punches, do you?"

"No, not in this, not now," she muttered, "not anymore. You wanted the truth before, and I didn't tell you. Well, the truth is, I don't think she loved you. I think she was hoping that she could love you, hoping that you could be the answer, but you weren't, and she wasn't prepared to figure out why or how to change the outcome. I don't know that she cared enough about anything at that point. She wanted a family, and she chose you as a sire, then found out that she was the one with the problem. Beyond that, she couldn't even think. I think she reacted, and you and I and various others were a casualty of her own chaos."

He didn't say anything as the elevator rose.

"What? Will you just randomly guess where we're going?"

He looked at her, then pointed out the energy on the elevator buttons. "Can you see it?"

"No, I can't. I can't see anything. What are you talking about?"

"The eight button had been pushed before I pushed it."

She stared at the buttons, even leaning closer to look. With a shrug, she stepped back and shook her head. "I can't see anything."

"I see the familiar energy on this button," he replied. "So, whoever we're chasing after is on the eighth floor."

When the door opened on the eighth floor, she stared out into the hallway and then followed Riff into the hall. She looked around. "Now what?"

"I follow the energy," he said, and he proceeded down the hallway until he stopped in front of a door. At that, he looked over at her and then rapped with some force on the door. When it opened a few minutes later, a woman looked up at him, terror etched on her face. "What?"

"I'm looking for the man who just arrived," he replied, giving her and the apartment behind her a hard glance.

"Nobody just arrived," she snapped.

"Yeah? Then let me in and prove it."

"I'll call the cops," she cried out, trying to shut the door.

"You can call the cops all you want," Riff stated, "but I think a murderer is in here. So the cops would be more than happy to tear apart your place to get him. You don't want to be harboring a murderer. That won't go well for you."

She stared at him in shock. "What are you talking about?" she asked, her words barely audible. "Nobody here is a murderer. My brother came for a visit. That's it."

"Then let me talk to him," Riff suggested, glaring at her. "Because we're following a murder inquiry, and he popped up."

"No, no, no," she said, almost hysterically. "No way. He

wouldn't have had anything to do with it."

"Prove it to me, and let me talk to him."

Just then a young man appeared behind her, glaring at them both. "What are you talking about?" he asked. "I didn't have nothing to do with nothing."

"So why did you run?" the woman asked him.

He swallowed hard and glared at her, then turned to address the strangers at the front door. "You didn't have to follow me here. This doesn't include my sister."

"If you avoided talking to us, we had to follow you, now didn't we?"

He shook his head. "I got nothing to say to you guys."

"Tell him it's not true," the sister said, turning to him. "Chip, … tell him it's not true."

"Now that we know who you are, that'll help," Riff pointed out, with a wolfish grin.

Chip glared at Riff, then turned to his sister. "Shut your mouth."

"No, I won't. What the hell are they talking about?" she asked, getting in his face, standing up on her tiptoes to even look him in the eye. "What the hell have you done now?"

"I didn't do nothing," he repeated. "You know that."

"No, I don't know that at all," she snapped. "You were supposed to not get into any more trouble. That was the condition for me helping you out."

He continued to glare at her. "I didn't get into any trouble. These guys don't know what the hell they're talking about, and, if you hadn't told them who I was, they wouldn't even know that much."

Suddenly she turned and looked at them.

"All you did was confirm his name," Angela noted. "We've been looking for Chip since he ran out the back of that pawn shop."

At that, the sister spun around and looked at him. "What the hell were you doing back there again? You told me you were done with that shit." Her fury erupted as she poked him in the chest. "You told me that you were done with that. Why the hell were you there?"

"I didn't have any money. I just went and did a few jobs for him."

"He's bad news, Chip. You know that," she cried out. "How many fucking times do I have to tell you to get away from him?"

"When you say, *bad news*," Riff interjected, "what kind of bad news are we talking?" His tone was quiet as he pushed Angela inside and joined her in the apartment, closing the door behind him.

She turned to the strangers. "Pawn shop bullshit, stolen goods, that whole crap."

"Hey, hey, hey," Chip said, "you don't get to tell him that."

"Why not?" his sister asked, glaring at him. "You promised me."

He continued to glare at her. "I've still got to make some money, don't I? You still want help with the rent."

"You're living here for free. Remember that, asshole? I told you that I would help you, but you're supposed to get a clean job and go straight, not turn around and crawl back into the same damn hole you were in before."

He held up his hands in a placating manner, but she wasn't having any of it.

She poked him in the chest again. "Now that I know you've been back there, these guys can talk to you all they want. Then you'll pack up your shit, and you're getting out of here. I don't want that same bullshit in my house ever again."

"No, no, no, come on, Amy. Don't do that to me," he cried out.

"Yeah, you can damn well bet I'll do that to you," she spat, barking mad. "You know what we agreed on, and you promised me that you were done with it."

"How am I supposed to get a job when nobody will hire me?" he asked, desperation in his tone.

"Maybe if you weren't hanging around with that piece of shit, you could get a job," she cried out. "I sent you to lots of places. Why didn't they hire you?"

"I don't know," he bellowed. "Besides, I'm not a dishwasher for crying out loud. I can't wash dishes."

"You mean, you don't want to make an honest living. That's what you're saying," she corrected. "That's a completely different story."

His shoulders slumped, and he nodded. "Fine, I'll go wash dishes then, but you know I made more money at the pawn shop."

"You made more money stealing shit," she cried out. "Other people's shit, people who got jobs as dishwashers, people who tried hard to make a go of it. Then you turn around and steal their shit, so they have to work longer at dishwashing jobs just to replace the shit you stole from them." She shook her head. "Christ, Chip. Mama would be so pissed at you right now."

"You won't tell her, will you?" he asked, his voice cracking.

She snapped, "Why the hell shouldn't I? She's the one who wanted me to give you a chance, one more try, one more time to go straight and to figure shit out." She shook her head. "Now, what do you do? You turn around, and you tie yourself to me again, and you don't go straight at all," she declared in complete disgust.

She turned to the two strangers in her home. "I don't know what the hell he did. He got a bad rap, but he was supposed to go clean," she turned and glared at her brother again. "You can see how well that worked out."

"Don't give up on me," Chip cried out desperately.

Angela winced, noting that he'd made a lot of life decisions that were probably shady, but that didn't mean he was a murderer. "How many bad decisions have you made?" Angela asked, staring at him. "Because we're talking murder right now, and that has a pretty high price tag."

He shook his head. "No murder, no, no," he said. "You're not pinning that shit on me. I didn't have nothing to do with it."

"Maybe not," Angela replied, "but you know who did, and we need that information."

He paled, looked at his sister, and almost lost his cool. "No, no, no. I can't talk, no way. He's powerful. More powerful than anybody else. I'll be dead in a heartbeat."

Amy snorted. "I can't believe you're still alive as it is," she muttered. "You keep screwing people over, hurting people, expecting everybody to forgive you. Then, when this shit comes down, you wonder why the hell I didn't want to have you back here again. Like what the hell, Chip?" She threw herself on the couch, glaring at him. "You brought this shit to my door. You think I want that?" she cried out, glaring at him.

Chip wailed, "Honest, it wasn't me." He turned and looked at the two of them. "I don't know how the hell you even pinned me for this, but it wasn't me."

"Maybe not," Angela conceded, "but I'm pretty damn sure, if we tested your DNA, we'll find it was you in that motel room that right, where two people were murdered. Somehow you survived."

At that, he went pale and collapsed beside his sister, staring up at them. His bottom lip trembled, and he started to cry.

His sister glared at him. "Jesus Christ, murder?" she repeated. "Did you really fall that far? … You offed two people?" she asked him in horror. He shook his head but couldn't talk, he was sobbing so badly. The sister started crying herself.

At that, Angela looked over at Riff. "Now what?"

A sudden stillness come over him. As she opened her mouth to ask him what was going on, he caught her off guard and threw her to the ground, covering her with his own body. She didn't have time to process anything, just as the air was split by gunfire.

RIFF BOLTED TO his feet and was at the shattered apartment door in seconds, running down the hallway to the stairwell, taking the stairs two at a time as he tried to outrun the shooter, who was at least a few minutes ahead of him. By the time, he hit the ground floor and raced out the front door, the getaway vehicle took off ahead of him. Swearing, he tried to sort out as much as he could, but it was just a small silver car, one of a thousand on the road right now. He couldn't even catch sight of the license plate.

With his phone in his hand, he called Terkel. "Gunfire at the apartment we're at," he began, not giving Terk a chance to ask anything. He searched the road signs near him. "Send an ambulance to the eighth floor, and, if you can, track a small gray car that just left the corner of Timberson and Corry. That's the shooter, as far as I can tell." Riff added, "We also need the street cams, if any face this apartment building." Then he gave the address.

"On it," Terkel replied, his tone terse. "Are you okay?"

"I am, yes, and I believe Angela is too," he replied, "but two other people are in that apartment, and we'll need the cops here as well." And, with that, he ended the call and raced back upstairs. Back in the apartment, he found Angela sitting beside the sister, who was sobbing in her arms.

"Is she okay?" Riff asked, as he walked inside.

She looked over at him and nodded, then pointed toward Amy's brother.

Riff winced because some bullets had hit true. Chip had taken two in the chest, and he was lying there, flung back in his chair, his mouth open, looking stunned at this turn of events. Riff walked over to the sister and crouched in front of her. "Are you physically hurt? Are you in any pain?"

She looked up at him, her eyes teary, and shook her head. "I tried so hard to stop him from coming to this damn end," she muttered, ultimately angry and crying. "Yet it seems as if nothing we did ever worked."

Riff nodded as he looked over at the brother. "I'm sorry. With his death also dies our answers."

At that, Amy looked up at him. "Did he really kill somebody?"

Riff replied, "Our information says he was at the murder scene."

Angela added, "His DNA was all over it. My sister was murdered there."

Amy started to sob again. "Damn him, damn him, damn him," she muttered. "How do I tell my mother this?"

Riff had no answer for that. He looked over at Angela, who seemed to be struggling with that one too.

"I'm sorry," Angela replied. "It's never easy to watch our family make decisions that hurt so many other people."

The sister just continued to sob.

It wasn't long before sirens neared them. Riff walked to the door, where the manager of the apartment complex stood, staring, then screamed at him, "What the hell happened here?"

He shrugged. "I don't know. Somebody opened fire. And, worse than that, we've got a dead man in here."

The manager stared behind him into the room, swallowed nervously, and muttered, "Well, shit."

"Yeah, *well, shit.*"

At that, the manager glared at him and announced, "I'll talk to her. This is BS."

"You'll have a talk with whom?" Riff asked, eyeing the manager with interest. "You're blaming the occupant of the apartment?" he asked incredulously.

"If she hadn't gotten into trouble, none of this would have happened," he snarled.

"Considering she's dealing with the loss of her brother right now, I sure wouldn't be too inclined to jump into that theory," he warned, his tone hard. "You can't blame her for anything Chip did."

"Sure, I can," he retorted, still glaring, but he was interrupted as the elevators opened, and paramedics and police officers rushed in. He stepped aside, glaring at Riff, who just shook his head.

"I wouldn't be making trouble for her right now," he

muttered, his tone very, very soft.

"Why is that?" the manager asked, trying to bluff his way through it.

"Because that'll piss me off," he replied. "I think she's been through enough." At that, Riff looked over at the cops and nodded toward the landlord. "He just threatened to evict her from her apartment because somebody else shot it up," he shared. "I highly doubt that would be considered normal behavior."

The cops turned to him, and the manager started to back off. "Hey, I was just upset about the property damage. The owners of the building won't be very happy to hear what's going on here."

"All of which has absolutely nothing to do with her," Riff added.

The manager nodded, yet kept backing up. "Fine, but, if it happens again, that's a different story." Then he turned tail and ran.

At that, one of the cops looked at him and asked, "Are you Riff?"

Riff nodded. "Yeah, I am, and I can tell you what happened, at least somewhat. It happened a little too fast for anyone to do anything but react." Then he went over the scenario with the cops. When Angela joined them, he instinctively held out a hand for hers, then pulled her in close. "She was in there with me, as was the sister of the victim."

"Do you think just the victim was the intended target?"

He looked at the cop who'd asked the question. "I'm not sure, but my guess would be yes. Although Angela and I could also potentially be targets."

The cop studied him in surprise. "You want to explain?"

Riff went over as much as he could. When the cop started to push him for more, Riff added, "You'll have to talk to Jonas over at MI6 for any further clarification, if that's not enough."

The cop just nodded, then turned to Angela. "So, you're looking into your sister's murder with this new information, and it led you here, correct?"

"Yes, that's right," she agreed. By the time they were done telling everything they could, Riff felt his own stress level starting to melt deeper and deeper into his bones. By the time they were allowed to go, with the interrogation complete and the body removed, apparently the mother of the victim had arrived as well, but Riff had missed that.

Emerging from the chaos, suddenly he stood outside in the hallway with Angela at his side, and everybody else was gone. He looked around. "Wow, I guess that's it, *huh?*"

"I guess. I sure don't feel like going back in that apartment again."

He looked at the makeshift door and nodded in understanding. "I don't think Chip's mother and sister will welcome us just now either." He led her slowly toward the elevators.

"I would rather walk," she said, "anything to get my mind off what just happened."

"That shifted pretty fast, didn't it?"

"And yet"—she gave him a searching gaze—"it's almost as if you knew it was coming, as if you were ready for it before it happened."

"I did, but only seconds before," he confirmed, his voice low. "I just got a feeling of something completely wrong, and that's when I tossed you to the floor and dove down after you. I couldn't cover everybody, and I had no idea that Chip was even in the line of fire."

"You're right though," she noted. "The shooter could have been targeting us too."

"That was quite likely the hope, you know, that they spray the room and get us all," he murmured. "We don't know whether Chip was the intended victim or it didn't matter to them, as long as they took us out."

"The gunman missed us and got Chip, but I still don't quite understand what that was all about."

"I suspect it'll be somebody Chip knew."

"You think it's the pawn shop guy?"

Riff shook his head. "I think the pawn shop guy knew an awful lot about it, and it might have been him, but I suspect, if we were at the pawn shop right now, he would be there too."

"So, in other words, not him."

"Maybe not him but I really want to know if he has a sibling."

"Oh," she said, startled. "That would make sense. You mentioned the familiarity of someone's energy. I just thought you meant Chip."

Riff shook his head. "What if the pawn shop owner has been covering for his brother or some relative, all these years?"

"You've got to wonder at what point in time the owner would stop doing that."

They hit the main floor and walked out the back of the apartment building, where their vehicle was parked. "You handled Amy really well back there," he shared, with a look of admiration.

"I have a little experience in delivering bad news and dealing with loss," she noted softly. "And a little bit of experience in trying to accept the poor behavior of someone you care about."

He squeezed her shoulder. "You're ahead of me there."

"No, I'm not," she argued. "You've done really well in such a short amount of time, and I certainly don't see that you have anything to work on."

"Maybe, but all this other stuff? … I don't know about the *witch* talk."

She nodded. "Anybody who understands energy work would say the same thing."

"It's frustrating." As they neared their vehicle, Riff stiffened, then pulled her tightly against him. "Look out."

Just then a cold voice behind them said, "Keep walking."

He stiffened a little more and shook his head. "Why should I keep walking?" He felt the snub end of a handgun pressed against his spine.

"Because, if I pull the trigger right now, you'll be a paraplegic for the rest of your life, assuming you survive," the man said, a harsh edge to his tone.

Even as Riff tried to stop her, Angela spun in his arms to turn and glare at the tall older man behind him. "Why the hell would you try to kill him?" she cried out. "You just killed Chip, so what more are you after?"

At that, the man behind Riff laughed. "Chip's dead, is he? That's not a bad thing. That kid's pathetic. He kept running home to his mom and sister every time he got into trouble. The kid never could stand on his own two feet."

"So, he needed a little more time to grow up," she stated in that same tone that Riff had seen her reserve for him, before all this happened. "What does any of this have to do with Sadie?"

Hearing that name, he sucked in his breath.

Riff slowly turned to stare at the gunman. "Well, well, well," he muttered, his voice soft. The gunman glared at him. "I don't suppose you are related to the pawnshop owner we just spoke to, are you?"

At that, Angela piped up, "You've got to be a relative. Are you the uncle of the new owner?"

He glared at her. "You looking for a bullet too?"

She shrugged. "We talked to the guy behind the counter earlier, who told us his parents died and left the shop to him. Supposedly he was the owner. Plus Chip was in the back room. What are the chances that you were in the back room too?"

He laughed. "I wasn't, but Chip called me soon enough afterward. The fact that he even called me in a panic told me how dangerous he was to leave lying around, like a loose cannon," he shared, with a headshake. "Since I'm gonna kill you both soon, I might as well share my brilliant plans with you. I've been setting up these networks of at least a dozen local thieves who work for me," he announced in a business-like tone. "Expendable people. They hit the houses, used my brother's shop for some of the goods, and a lot of the rest? … Well, I work privately with a bigger international network that I've taken a lot of trouble to set up," he noted, his voice raspy from his growing anger. "So, you coming into the pawn shop put a target on your backs. And the mention of a diary? … So like that stupid bitch," he snapped, his ire rising. "What the hell was she thinking, putting that shit on paper?"

"You mean, the fact that she loved Johnny?" Angela asked.

"I doubt it," he argued, followed by a laugh. "That woman didn't love anybody but herself. Once she got more into the drugs and alcohol, she became a loose cannon herself. I don't know who flipped that switch in her world, but she got worse and worse," he told them. "She came on to me, and, if she wanted something from the shop, she would come on to my brother. Toward the end, she came on to anybody. She didn't care. It's like she had a death wish. If she couldn't have what she wanted, she didn't give a crap. She'd stopped being the person everybody thought she was and become this really odd duck," he described, with a headshake. "I didn't understand her at the end, but I'll tell you one thing. … What I did understand was that she was dangerous."

"Is that why you killed her?" Riff asked. "I mean, it's not as if she was any real danger to you. You were fairly well protected behind your networks."

"I was and I wasn't," the gunman replied. "I didn't have much of a chance to get everything in place back then. I was just positioning things. She could have screwed things up royally. She kept threatening to expose me. Once she was drunk, all she could talk about was the fact that she could do things."

"What kind of things?" Riff asked.

"Things that could … mess me up," he stated, "and I would never even know it. I tried to talk to her about it, to ask her what she was talking about. She wouldn't say any more. I got her drunk one night to see if I could get her to open up about it a little. She used to play with the men around her. It was some energy game," he said. "She could make them all want her really badly. Then, when they were under her spell, she would do whatever the hell she wanted with them."

Riff stiffened at that and glared at him. "You believed

her?"

"Hell, I watched her do it, over and over, man. She had some charisma going on that I didn't get, but I was immune to it. Once I'd seen her work it, … no way I would fall for that BS. She tried it a couple times on me, but it was a hell no."

"She was good at it?" Riff asked.

"Yeah, but only for those who didn't understand what she was doing. The minute you knew what she was doing, she couldn't get it past you. Once you were sucked into believing her bullshit, you couldn't see straight. Johnny was hooked. He couldn't see straight, being the bloody mess that he was." He shook his head. "That was just fucking dangerous, and she was weird."

"Yeah, tell me about it," Angela muttered. "And here I figured you were into all that same stuff yourself."

He shook his head. "No, I used to let her think I was though. It was the best way to keep her in control because, if she thought that I was part of the whole hocus-pocus bullshit, then she would show me a little more about what she could do. But what the hell do you do with that? Even crazy needs controlling, and she was flipping out."

"Did she ever tell you anything about her family?"

"Yeah, something about having screwed her sister's fiancé as a lesson to her sister about making sure she fell in love with the right person—or at least that she was in love with him or some bullshit. She told me that she did it to teach her sister a lesson." He snorted. "Who does that to their own sister?" he asked, with yet another headshake.

"Somebody who's deeply unhappy," Angela replied.

At that, he narrowed his gaze at her and then burst out laughing. "That was you, wasn't it?" he asked, a smile cracking his face. "Christ, how you must have loved her."

"Not particularly, not at all."

"Who was it that you were in love with that you didn't want anybody to know about? Because that's what she was all about. She figured you would do something with somebody else. Sadie mentioned how she was all wrong for him but how you were all right."

At that, she glared at him. "She was crazy at the end."

Riff ignored the look on her face but couldn't ignore her tone of voice. Then he realized exactly what was going on there between the sisters. He groaned and asked her, "Seriously?"

She shrugged. "What do you want me to say? As far as she was concerned, doing what she did was her way of pointing me in the right direction."

"Why? Because she couldn't break up with me?"

"I don't think she could do it. I think she needed you to break up with her, so she didn't have to make that decision."

"Also, that way she was the victim," the gunman pointed out, laughing at Riff. "You've got the right sister now. Jesus, look at this? Here we've got the fiancé and the sister. Both of you are bloody nuts, but then so was Sadie," he declared, turning to look at the sister. "Are you as creepy crazy as she was?"

"No. That was my sister, and she got a whole lot worse with the drugs."

"You got that right," he agreed. "Never saw anybody have such bad trips as she did. I told her that she should stop taking the stuff, that it disagreed with her, but she wouldn't listen. Not only would she not listen, she wouldn't even give you the time of day. If you told her to stop, she would turn around and take a double dose. A couple times I thought she would OD on us."

"Yet she hid it from everybody else," Riff noted, frowning at him.

"You were never around to see it, though she said she preferred it that way," he noted, with a laugh. "It was much easier to keep up the façade."

"But why a façade?" Angela asked. "I don't get that. I mean, why go to all the effort?"

"Something about kids," he said, with a wave of the gun still pointed in Riff's face. "I told her that she wouldn't get my fucking seed, no way. If I ever had a kid, I would confirm the mother was somebody not crazy, like she was."

"I'm sure she loved that," Angela muttered. "She couldn't have kids, and that may be behind all this *crazy*, but it still seems to be such an over-the-top reaction."

"Had you seen your sister lately?" the gunman asked, sneering. "She was over-the-top always."

"How long had you known her?" Riff asked.

"A long time, and she was always that way. Sure, she'd be calm for a while, but then she'd get into a mood again. She would start fights, cause fights, cause people to take off on her and leave her all alone. Then she would hook up with another guy. Yet, when she was with you," the gunman added, turning to Riff, "she figured she had it made, until she found out about the damn kids."

The gunman shook his head. "I told her to fuck off about the kids, that nobody gave a shit, and how enough unwanted kids were in this world already. So she sure as hell shouldn't be having any, especially not in the mental state she was in."

"So, she was always a little off?" Riff asked, staring at him. "I didn't see it."

"No, you didn't see it, but you didn't see much of her, did you?"

Riff slowly shook his head.

The gunman nodded. "That's because she could only be stable for so long. Whatever that bloody energy work she was always going on about, … every time she used it, there was a price to pay, and she had to be somebody else for a while afterward—like when she was with you. Then she would be really good for a while, but she couldn't handle it for long. So she would go kick up the town, and she always did it in such a way that she ended up making shitty decisions."

Turning back to Angela, the gunman added, "Like sleeping with your fiancé. Christ, you probably forgave her too, didn't you? One of those fucking bloody know-it-all do-gooders," he muttered, with a snarl.

"Oh, I loved my sister, but I didn't love her that much," Angela responded. "Obviously it hurt like shit for her to do that. So forgiveness from me? Not yet."

"Yeah, and she laughed at you all the time, said you wouldn't do anything you needed to do for yourself. Part of that was because of what she'd done to you. Something about camouflaging what you could do because you were stronger than her, but you were hindered by a conscience, and she wasn't." He snorted. "I overheard bits and pieces over time. She kept your energy snuffed down so you didn't know what she could do. After she'd expended a lot of her energy on shitty stuff, she had to go to the *source of all goodness*." He gave a mocking laugh.

"Meaning you, and soak up all that loving energy before Sadie could go on to the next thing. Didn't you ever wonder how she was tired and worn out with you and then felt much better as she left your presence?"

"Sure, but she was my sister. Of course she'd come to unwind. I always helped to make her feel better."

At that, he burst out laughing. "She manipulated you, just as she did everyone else. I remember one time she said it was up to her to confirm you did the right thing. I don't know what that was though, and she was full of that shit. She even slept with one of Johnny's girlfriends, just to point out to him that he needed her. Johnny knew she was messed up, but he was just as crazy as everybody else. If you ask me, I was the only sane one in the lot."

"Yet I thought everybody was talking about you doing witchy stuff?" Angela noted.

"No, that was BS. Sadie started getting into rituals and all that, so I bought her a few things as a joke. When I saw this vial of blood on the ground outside the hospital— probably a lab sample that someone must have dropped—I brought it to her. She thought it was the best thing ever, almost swooning with joy over it. I tell you it was freaking sick. Then some of the shit she talked about was beyond sick too. I sure hope she couldn't really do what she boasted she could do."

Angela turned to Riff. "I didn't see any of that."

"Neither did I," he replied, "but he's right. We didn't see very much of her at the end there, did we?"

"Not after the fight I had with her. That wasn't all that long after she found out she couldn't have kids. I tried to talk to her, but she wasn't into it."

The gunman snorted. "You could have talked until you were blue in the face, and it wouldn't have made a damn bit of difference with Sadie. I'm telling you that she was nuts. But nuts in a way that was slowly disintegrating. You would think that she was totally okay. Everybody else would think she was totally okay because, on the surface, she was. ... However, the longer she went on trying to keep everybody from knowing who she really was, she was unraveling on the inside, and she got worse and worse. You should have been fucking happy that I took her out."

She stared at him. "You think I should have been happy that you killed my sister, when all she needed was a bit of help?"

"Crazy like that can only be helped when you take them out to the back alley and shoot them in the head," he declared. "So, yeah, I think you owe me. She's been doing shit to you for years, and you never knew because somehow she could use the love you had for her to camouflage her actions—or some shit like that."

So much of what they'd just learned made a lot of sense, not just in regard to Angela's energy and supposed lack of abilities but also why Riff himself hadn't seen what was right in front of him when it came to Sadie.

Riff studied the gunman shifting from side to side in front of him. "And then you shot Chip. Did you also kill Johnny?"

"Sure. He was right there. Why not?"

"What about James Teespawl?"

"No, I didn't have to. Somebody in jail took care of that."

"You got that kind of influence?"

He burst out laughing, a big grin crossing his face. "Anything I want in prison I can get," he stated. "All you need is money, and believe me that I've got money. But ain't no way I'm letting you guys mess up what it took me so long to get set up," he stated, glaring at them. "It's bullshit to even think I would risk losing all of that."

"So, you had to kill Chip?" Angela asked.

"He was a loser anyway, and sometimes, with losers, you just can't do nothing about it. In his case, … Chip would never amount to anything."

"Which is another judgment that you really don't get to make for other people," Angela snapped.

"Yeah?" he quipped, giving her a sly grin. "What will you do about it? Unless you'll do some of that woo-woo energy stuff that your sister was all about."

Riff nodded, turning to Angela. "Considering Sadie was blocking your energy and stifling your growth on that front, chances are, you'll soon feel a ton of fresh and totally freeing energy surge through you, now that you know. It's one thing to dampen energy while the person trusts you and has no clue. It's another thing entirely to keep doing it now that she's dead and gone. Plus, you have the facts now, Angela. You've kept Sadie alive in your heart and in your soul, out of guilt, needing to find out who killed her, but you know all that now …"

He smiled, seeing her energy stretch upward at his words, bigger than her physical body, softer and wispier, until full power started to surge through her. Shocked, she twisted to him, and he nodded. "That energy was always there, sweetheart. You let Sadie do that to you. But now you know better, and you can throw off the shackles of a lifetime and really come into your own power. Just think of all the healing you can do with just a little bit of training. And we know who can help you there."

"Healing?" the asshole spat. "Figures you would do something along the do-gooder route."

She smiled at the gunman a little too sweetly, putting Riff immediately on alert, even as he watched her shrug, almost as if pulling on a new suit and settling it in place. It was in her stance, in the tilt of her head, in the glint in her eye. This was the Angela she'd always longed to be.

She kept smiling at their gunman. "I can do a couple things that you won't understand, and you would probably think was pretty woo-woo."

"Yeah, like what?" he asked, jeering at her, taunting her.

"I can snap my fingers in your face and drop you to your knees. Something to do with meridian lines. Right now, of course, I'm not in full control of my energy," she whispered in a confidential manner. "So it might work a little too well."

He stared at her and paled. "Hell, no way," he cried out. "I'm too fucking strong for a little thing like you."

Even as the gunman glared at her, Riff noted the fear in the gunman's gaze. It wouldn't take much to drop him just because of that fear. Fear made him a victim. Being a victim made him weak.

She snapped her fingers in front of his face, and he dropped to his knees, his gun along with it, and he froze in place, completely incapable of doing anything but stare at her in shock. She smiled. "How is that for a demonstration?"

He opened his mouth, but nothing came out. When he repeatedly tried to speak, and nothing worked, he just stared at her in shock.

She nodded. "People can do all kinds of shit in the energy world," she shared. "So don't ever mock my sister. She was unstable but that's because she was so damn unhappy. I'm not excusing her for all the shit she pulled, but she doesn't need to be remembered in that way either. She was somebody who needed help. That's all, no more, no less."

Riff picked up the handgun from the alley pavement where it had fallen.

The gunman continued to work his mouth, which seemed to be the only body part he could control. When he gave up again, he just stared at her in shock.

She turned to Riff and asked, "Can we finally be done with this crap?"

As Riff was tying the hands of their prisoner, he turned to her. "If you can do this, how the hell did your sister do all that shit to you? It makes no sense."

"Yes, it does," she countered. "I trusted her. You heard our gunman say how Sadie wasn't able to get to him because he didn't trust her. I knew her. I loved her, and she was already part of my energy, so she could muck it up as much as she wanted to. … It's the worst kind of betrayal."

Riff nodded in understanding. "You're right, and I knew that, but the shock of seeing how quickly it pivoted was both beautiful and unnerving."

Their prisoner began to move, trying to get to his feet, even while shackled. "Your spell wore off, bitch. Wow, Sadie really screwed you over good, didn't she?" Their prisoner started to laugh. "Serves you guys right. If you can fucking do shit like that, you shouldn't be allowed to live." He glared at her. "I should have popped you one too."

"You can try," she said in a cheerful tone. Hearing sirens in the distance, she asked Riff, "Are those for us?"

He nodded. "They sure are." He shoved the gunman against his vehicle, his cheek pressed against the roof. "I want to confirm this guy gets put away."

"Won't matter if I am or not," he grumbled. "You won't get me for anything."

"You just confessed that you killed my sister," Angela pointed out. "So I'm pretty sure we can get you for that and for Johnny's murder and Chip's and James Teespawl too."

"Doesn't matter," he snapped. "I'll get out in a few years, and hear me well. … I'll find you."

She gave him a hard look. "No, you won't." He turned and stared at her, his gaze narrowing. "Unless you want me to blind you right now," she said very softly.

His eyes widened in alarm. "Hell no," he muttered. "What the fuck?"

"Then don't threaten me," she said coolly. "You don't know what the hell I can do, what he can do, what any of us can do," she pointed out. "And, if you mention it to anybody, they'll just think you're off your rocker. They'll section you. Then you can just sit back and wait for the moment when *we* come find you."

He glared at her.

"You know I'm right," she stated, nodding. "Too bad you didn't find a way to use my sister's talents for the good."

"You couldn't use her talents for anything," he muttered. "I tell you that she was messed up. She was beyond helping. She was a loser, and I don't spend time with losers."

"Guess what?" Angela said softly. "That's about to change because a whole lot of inmates are waiting to meet you." She smiled. "I'll be sure to put in a special word."

Just then the cops pulled in, and it took a bit, but some explanations were given, some phone calls made, and then finally the gunman was taken away in a cop car.

As she stood outside in the same alleyway, looking at Riff, she shook her head. "This feels very anticlimactic somehow."

He nodded thoughtfully. "It does, doesn't it?"

She hesitated. "Is it over? I mean, could anybody else even be involved?"

"I don't know," he admitted, as he turned to look

around for a minute. "Did the previous pawn shop owner have a brother?"

Angela shrugged. "The cops will figure that out. Do you really think our gunman, if he is the uncle, had any way of keeping all this from his brother? Or … shit. Maybe his brother found out, and our gunman killed his own brother," she suggested.

"It's possible. This old guy had quite a few notches in his gun belt that we heard of just tonight." Riff pointed at their vehicle. "The guys are back at the hotel, so let's reconvene and see how we're doing."

She nodded and smiled. "I'll be more than happy to have this day over with. A shower would also be lovely."

As they headed back to the hotel, he added, "Maybe we should call ahead and see about dinner."

She shrugged. "Or, once we get there, we can just order in, and I can get my shower in the meantime."

"If that's what you want." He grinned at her. "So, how close was your sister's theory about *the right one*?"

She glared at him. "I really don't want to talk about it."

"Is it true?"

"None of your business," she muttered.

"So, it is true," he pressed, with a nod of satisfaction.

She glared at him. "Why? Would that make you happy?"

"Actually it makes me ecstatic," he declared, with a laugh. "You should think about that for a moment." She stared at him, and he laughed. "As if you need to really think about it."

CHAPTER 13

IT DIDN'T TAKE Angela long, and then it went *click*. "Seriously?" She stared at Riff, dumbfounded.

"Yeah," he confessed. "Why do you think I didn't care to be around her? I mean, I asked her if she wanted me to be home, but I wasn't pushing myself to be there. She was comfortable enough to be around, and I had somebody, but I wasn't all that anxious to close that loop and to seal the deal," he admitted, with a shrug. "I knew something was off, but I didn't want to do what it took to figure it out. For the first time in a long time, I had somebody there waiting for me, somebody who I thought maybe really cared," he added. "Now I realize it was just her way of manipulating the scenario, but, for a little while, I got sucked into it," he said, with a nod. "Can't say I want to go through that again."

"You and me both." Angela groaned. "It was damn unpleasant."

"And your fiancé?"

"He was a consolation prize for a time," she conceded.

He looked over at her, then flashed her a big grin. "So?"

"So what?" she asked crossly. "It's not exactly something I want to talk about."

"No, probably not, but the only reason Sadie would have done that, *as a lesson for you*, was if you were in love with me, and you didn't want to tell me."

"What would I say?" she asked in astonishment. "You were engaged to my sister."

He nodded. "Good point. We were both idiots."

"Yeah, we were," she agreed, "particularly if you're telling me now that you actually cared about me."

"I did. I was fascinated, but I was engaged to her and wasn't sure what to do about it. So I just avoided the whole issue."

"*Great*, that's mature."

He shot her a look and asked, "And your way was better?"

She shrugged. "Okay, so we both suck."

He burst out laughing. "That's one way to look at it, yeah. I figured you didn't want anything to do with me."

"Yeah, and that was probably my sister telling you that."

"I think it probably was actually," he admitted, frowning. "I don't remember ever having much of a regular conversation with her."

"I'm not surprised," she muttered. "That's the way she was. Yet you were attracted in the first place."

"Yeah, I was, as anyone would be. She was a very attractive woman, and she could be very charming, very sweet. I just didn't spend as much time with her as everybody else apparently. So I didn't really see the underbelly that she worked hard to conceal."

"Again, I think that underbelly was more because she was really unhappy. Possibly sick and getting worse every day while using her energy in a negative way. That shit's no good for us energy workers, but I also won't crucify her for it. She's dead and gone, and now we know how and why," she stated. "So I'll count that as a good day."

"I would too," he replied.

When they pulled into the hotel parking lot, she got out, and, at his side, they walked up to the hotel room. "Did you hear from the guys?" she asked.

He nodded. "While we were waiting for the cops, they texted, saying they were heading in."

"Good." She yawned. "It's been one hell of a day. I'll fill everybody in, have a shower, and then just crash."

"What will you do after this?"

"Go back, check on some babies and their mothers. After that? … I don't know," she said. "I am serious about learning more about healing via energy work. I think it would be good for me."

"I think it would be good for you too," he said softly. "Besides, … I think we need to spend some time together."

She laughed. "You mean, you don't know enough about me already?"

"I do," he stated, as they got to the hotel room. He pushed it open, grinning down at her. "I just never thought it was reciprocated."

"Well, well, well," said a man with a hard tone from a dark corner. "Isn't that cute? Two lovebirds."

She stiffened as the door slammed behind her, cutting off their escape. And there, a sly grin on his face, was another older man. His energy matched their gunman in the alleyway. Damn. Brothers. This could be the supposedly dead father who left the pawn shop to the guy behind the counter. Energy doesn't lie.

Fury slid through her, finding them in this same life-and-death situation all over again. This guy also held a handgun on Riff. Meanwhile, she noted Royce and Langdon, who were tied up and slouched on the couch—unconscious, she hoped. Her gaze went from one to the other and back to the real pawn shop owner. "Good God." She stomped into the center of the room. "Haven't I had enough of you and your damn family drama?"

He looked at her in astonishment.

"That bloody brother of yours, what a waste of space he is," she snapped, just starting to rip into her tirade.

He frowned at her and then at Riff. "She better shut up."

"Yeah, well, shutting her up isn't all that easy," he said, with a slight laugh. "You've got to admit your brother is a waste of space."

He glared at him. "What the hell did he do now?"

"He shot and killed Chip for one."

At that, his jaw dropped. "He what?"

"Yeah," Angela confirmed, "and right in front of Chip's poor sister, for Christ's sake. Shot up the entire apartment like he didn't think he would get caught."

At that, the gunman stared at them with suspicion. "No, he wouldn't be so stupid."

"*Yeah*? He *was* that stupid, and the cops have him in custody already," Riff declared, taking two steps forward.

The gunman raised the handgun. "Oh, no you don't, not another step." He looked over at Angela. "You get over here and sit down beside these two."

Instead, she walked directly toward him, and he held the gun at her threateningly.

"That's enough out of you," he said, followed by a biting laugh. "Believe me that I've just about had it with you and that sister of yours. The things she could do was one thing, but only when she was clear of mind, and too often … she wasn't even that. I don't know if you can do the same damn things she could or not, but you can bet I won't give you a chance to try."

At that, she stared at him. "So, you're the one who's into the esoteric stuff."

He shrugged. "I saw her do some pretty amazing things," he said. "So I know it's possible. I just don't know who all can do it and whether you being family means you have the same abilities." This gunman looked over at Riff. "Sadie told me that he couldn't do anything, just thought he could."

At that, Riff gave him a lazy smile. "You could never really trust what she said, remember?"

"I didn't realize at the beginning that she was serious, but I tell you, man oh man, could she make a roomful of men move. If that woman wanted to charm a room, … she sure as hell could do it," he stated. "Yeah, she charmed me for a while, but it was more a fascination with everything else she had going on that I was interested in. Man, to learn those tricks and to have people open their wallets and just do what I needed them to do? It's damn addicting."

He laughed. "Sadie was fucking perfect, but she couldn't seem to teach me. I wanted to take off with her and just spend some one-on-one time to figure out what I needed to learn to make it happen myself. She kept telling me that she could teach me, promised to teach me, but she didn't. Finally, when I realized that she was just full of hot air, I sicced my brother on her, and, boy, did he go to town."

"Doing what?" Angela whispered, and Riff saw the air around her aura move ever-so-slightly.

"Hell, I didn't really think he would do what he did, but, man, when he got pissed off at her, he just took out his frustration on her in a big way," he shared. "He threatened Johnny but then just took him out. No telling how he would react now that Sadie was dead. Chip was there too at the time, but my brother went in with a hood on, and nobody knew anything. My brother intended to kill them all. Somehow Chip didn't die. I think the experience changed Chip in a big way afterward. He wasn't quite the same anymore. Once he saw two people killed right in front of him, Chip went south. He went to jail for doing a bunch of stupid things.

"I didn't have much time for that stuff. I was too busy trying to keep my brother on the straight and narrow, while he worked his business angle. He always had a bigger idea, a big deal happening. Some of it was good. Some of it helped us a lot, but some of his ideas were just terrible. So, I had to constantly rein him in and make him do some actual business analysis before he got too deep into one of his plans."

The real pawn shop owner sighed. "Yet, man, when it came to that Sadie chick … he was pretty well into the hate. I was into the love, not of her but of what she could do, and, damn, could she do shit," he shared. "But like everything, you've got to be stable enough to work it, and she just wasn't balanced. Maybe all that bad woo-woo stuff did have a negative effect. I don't know. She was playing so many games, and it was screwing around so much in her head that she was starting to lose track of reality. She was a sad sight by the end," he added, looking over at the two of them.

"I'm really sorry she died. So Sadie was your sister and your fiancée," he confirmed, pointing to Angela first and then Riff. The gunman added an eye roll. "That's got to suck, man, particularly when you realize she was screwing around with Johnny at the time. But, as far as I know, it was only Johnny when she was engaged to you. She wasn't with me, and she wasn't with Chip or with my brother," he noted.

"So, I guess there's that good news to think of. Not a whole lot of that though. I'm sorry she's dead because I think she still could have taught me a lot. I was pretty pissed when I found out that my brother had done such a permanent number on her, but that's my brother. Always the extremist."

He shook his head and then stared hard at both of them. "Anyway, the problem now is that, according to what you guys are saying, my brother has once again screwed up, and I'm once again left to clean up his shit. I'm getting damn tired of it," he muttered.

"This time you'll have a much bigger problem because he'll go to prison for killing Sadie and Chip, plus Johnny," Riff added.

The gunman nodded at that thoughtfully. "Yeah, you're probably right. This might be the one time I need to clean house and maybe relocate to a better place in the world," he suggested, with a shrug. "You know what they say about family? You can't live with them, and you can't live without them," he said, with half a grin, looking at them both conspiratorially, thinking they would understand.

She glared at him. "My sister never got the chance to live, thanks to you and your brother."

"Whatever," he muttered, with a wave of the gun.

"What about these two? Did you hurt them?" She looked over at Langdon and Royce, still seemingly unconscious.

"Nope, sure didn't, but I did come in and take them down. One was just coming to the door, and I took him out first so I could grab the other one. You really don't want to face two of them at a time," he noted, with a whistle. "Now you? Well, you're not exactly much of a challenge, but I think the guy behind you would be a whole different story,"

He laughed. "So, I'm not taking any chances." He raised his gun and shot behind her. She spun, expecting to see Riff on the ground in pain, only to turn back and see the shooter staring at the empty space behind her.

"Where is he?" he roared. "Where did he go?"

She walked closer to her newest gunman, and, snapping her fingers in front of him, knocked the gun out of his hand.

He stared down at her in shock. "What the hell did you just do?" Then he belted her hard across the face. She cried out as she flew backward onto the ground, struggling to get to the gun before he got there first. Just as she snatched it up, he slammed his booted foot down on her hand. She cried out again, twisting underneath him, but he applied pressure until she couldn't do anything. He leaned over to grab the gun. "Nice trick, bitch."

As he went to pick up the gun, he went ass-over-teakettle as Riff booted him head-on. He was on him with a couple hard rights, another left, and then he flipped him over, until he was flat on his back, and gave him a few more hard crunches to the jaw for good measure. When the intruder stopped moving, Riff hopped up, flipped him over, pulled his hands behind his back, and looked over at her. "You want to see if we've got something to tie him up with?"

"He's got a belt on. Let's use that."

Together, they pulled off the intruder's belt and quickly secured him in place. Then she untied both Royce and Langdon. As she nudged them awake and helped them both up to their feet, she asked them in concern, "You guys okay?"

They just nodded and looked at her with an odd expression. "Yeah, we're fine. He caught us by surprise."

"There's a lot of that going on right now," she noted, with a wave of her hand. "We got taken by surprise outside

Chip's apartment by this guy's brother."

When their eyebrows shot up, she quickly explained, and Riff nodded. "When you go looking for one pawn shop owner, you don't expect to find two, much less three, which is what happened here," he said. "So, it looks as if we've got them all now. The whole damn family. At least the local cops should have secured the son back at the pawn shop by now."

She smiled, looking down at the unconscious man. "I hope they like being a family in jail together," she muttered. "Every damn one of them needs to go there."

Riff looked over at her and asked, "How's your face?"

She winced. "It'll be fine. It's sore, and so is my hand," she admitted, holding it up. "I hope he didn't break it. My fault. I'm not exactly in control of my renewed energy yet."

He walked over, examined her hand gently, and still she winced. He shook his head. "I don't think it's broken. You're moving it," he noted. "We'll keep an eye on it, and, if you want, we'll take you in for X-rays."

She snorted. "Hell no, I would rather go home and see if Clary can help."

"I'm sure she could," he replied, with a smile, "but not tonight." He looked over at Royce and Langdon. "You want to call it in? The cops are getting pretty-damn tired of me."

At that, Langdon laughed a little harder than he intended. "I will."

Riff smiled. "I'll contact Terkel and give him an update."

"Good enough," Langdon said.

Angela turned to Royce. "Meanwhile, you and I will decide on dinner."

He grinned at her and asked, "What have you got in mind?"

She shrugged. "I don't care as long as there's plenty of it, and it's hot, and it comes soon. ... I'm tired, worn out, and fed up. I want nothing more than a hot shower and a shit ton of food, and then I'll sleep for a week."

It didn't take them long to find a pizza place close by that delivered, and, with that ordered, she headed to the shower. When she came out dressed again, law enforcement officers were in the room.

Groaning, she asked, "Will this ever end?" She recognized one of the cops from earlier encounters with the local authorities, and he turned and glared at her. She raised both hands in mock surrender. "Hey, don't get mad at me," she said in exasperation. "This is your city, and you guys seem to suck at keeping it safe." When his jaw dropped in astonishment, she nodded. "I've been attacked how many times today? And I didn't do anything."

"Yet you're somehow managing to make all kinds of enemies."

She shrugged. "Some people just get pissed off over the littlest things."

The local authorities got their info and left soon afterward.

RIFF WALKED OVER to Angela and gave her a big hug. "How are you feeling?"

"Better," she muttered, "but I need food, and I need sleep. After that, I need all of this to stop."

"It has stopped," he declared.

The pizza arrived just then, changing the conversation and their focus. When they were done eating, she settled back, patted her tummy, and said, "Now, I just need to sleep for a week."

Riff smiled. "Go then."

She nodded. "Right, so, if you'll excuse me, guys, I'm done, so I'm crashing." She got up, headed to her bedroom, and closed the door on them.

Langdon looked over at Riff. "How was she?"

"She had the dandiest trick," he shared. "With a snap of her fingers, it froze the first brother for maybe a couple minutes, but it didn't repeat with this brother. She's still working to control her full-on energy that she has now. Still, her trick completely shifted this guy's energy just enough for her to get one up on him," he muttered, with a headshake.

At that, Royce nodded. "If it's done on the meridian line, it can completely disrupt the energy for just that fraction of a second. It's a good trick, and I was surprised she knew how to do it."

"She did it all right. I would say she has a handle on it because she used it twice, and it lasts longer than a fraction of a second too. It was damn effective." He looked over at the closed bedroom door in admiration.

"And now, with this over," Langdon added, "you can relax, chill, and get your life together."

Riff stopped for a moment and nodded. "It's such a strange feeling to know that I've been waiting for this for so long, and now that it's here? … I don't quite know what to think."

"And that's the point. Now that it's here, just relax and let time do its thing," he suggested.

"That's the plan. I think in the end, Sadie just couldn't handle the news that she couldn't have kids. She got to a place where she just didn't care anymore. … Not sure that she ever cared about me either, but one of the lovely realities that's come to light is that I'm not sure I cared enough about her either," he shared. "It's all pretty messed up."

Langdon nodded, giving Riff a huge smile. "And, like everything else in life, it needs time to get *not* messed up. So, relax a bit, don't put any pressure on yourself, and just chill."

He nodded and asked, "What about you guys?"

They looked at each other and back at him. "We'll head back, since this is over. We've got family at home. A chance to spend a little time with our partners and to sleep in our own beds tonight sounds pretty good right now," Royce admitted. "It's still pretty early, and the two of us can get there soon enough."

"We'll let them know you guys will be heading back to base in the morning," Langdon added in a soft tone.

"Good enough." Riff quickly helped them pack up, and soon they were gone. Now he was alone in a hotel room with Angela. He got up and opened the door to check on her, but she appeared to be sound asleep. He smiled as he went to close the door.

She whispered, "I'm not really asleep."

"Yes, you are," he said. "Go back to sleep."

"What about you?"

"I'm going to bed. This has been one hell of a deal, and I'm done for."

"It has been hell," she whispered. "You can sleep in here, you know?"

He froze at that, looked at the small form in the big bed, then added a little carefully, "That's probably a bad idea."

"Hell, we've had nothing but bad ideas for years, but I'm way too tired to do anything but sleep. And you've not slept this whole time, so you need it even worse than me. Besides, if you're in here, you won't be half awake, listening to confirm I'm okay. Hop in and get some real sleep."

And, with that, she pulled down the covers on the far side, rolled over a bit to give him her back, then quickly drifted to sleep again. He had a quick shower, still questioning the sensibility of sharing a bed with her, realizing that all kinds of things could end up happening, wondering if he was ready to head down that road, only to realize he'd been heading down that road for a very long time. He'd been looking for closure in order to give himself permission to explore this pathway and had yet to give it to himself.

And now, here was an invitation from her, at a point in time when he really was free to accept or decline as he chose. What he really wanted was to curl up in that bed, pull her into his arms, and sleep. After a long moment of drying off and checking to confirm the door was locked, he headed to her bed and curled up on the empty side.

Then he put an arm around her and pulled her up against him. When she mumbled something completely indecipherable, he whispered, "It's just me. Go to sleep."

As soon as he felt her breathing shift into a deep, slow state, he fell asleep right beside her.

CHAPTER 14

ANGELA WOKE TO what felt like a blazing fire wrapped around her. She froze here for a long moment, aware of who it was now, and just smiled, sinking deeper into his sleepy embrace. She didn't want to move, yet her bladder was getting insistent. Finally she eased herself out from under his arm and headed to the bathroom. When she came back out again, he was awake and looking up at her.

He pulled back the blanket. She immediately slipped under it. "Sorry if I woke you. I had to go to the bathroom," she admitted.

"Mother Nature usually wins those arguments," he noted, with a yawn. She smiled and agreed. "How did you sleep?" he asked, as he shifted to give her a bit more room.

"I slept pretty well, except for waking up, wrapped in a furnace."

He shrugged. "I'm always on the hot side of life."

"That's because you're hot," she muttered.

He looked over at her in surprise and then grinned. "Hang on a minute. Was that a compliment and not an insult? You aren't screaming at me, so I'm a little confused."

She flushed. "Yeah, we haven't exactly had a normal relationship, have we?"

"Nope, we sure haven't," he agreed, "and I'll say we haven't had a normal courtship either."

She winced. "Is that what it's been?"

"Sure, it has," he stated. "We've been dancing around it for weeks, months, years even, and I don't know how much of it was because of your sister and how much was just because we care."

She smiled. "I prefer to think it's because we care, yet weren't prepared to step in that direction."

"Yeah, me too," he confirmed, as he pulled her back into his arms. "I slept wonderfully, thank you. Nothing like being beside an angel to make me sleep soundly."

"Hardly an angel," she muttered, with an eye roll. "I'm pretty sure you've called me any number of names in the last five years or so, and not one of them was the least bit angelic."

He grinned. "Nope, but they kept you firmly on that side of the dividing line and out of bounds, so it did its job."

"*Right*," she grumbled, "like that's fair."

He laughed. "All's fair in love and war, remember?"

She smiled. "So, I'm really not sure which side of that we're on either."

"We are on the love side," he stated firmly. "I also think we've wasted more than enough time trying to avenge your sister's death. She was messed up, crazy, and needed help, and that's the consensus we're going with. So, we'll leave it be," he said. "Yet, if she felt so strongly about you needing to tell me how you felt, I wonder why she never said anything to me about it."

She shook her head. "I don't know. Maybe she just couldn't handle that much honesty and figured that pointing it out to me would make it easier on me. None of it quite makes sense. In a twisted way, I think she did care about you and figured that you weren't right for each other. She cared about me and figured that I was right for you instead, but probably couldn't let either one of us go down that pathway on our own because then she'd have to face the consequences of being alone on the other side, and that wouldn't be easy for her."

He nodded. "You know, that's good enough for us, and we don't need any further explanations. We'll try to remember her with joy and with peace, as the person we knew her to be when she was at her best," he offered.

Angela smiled and looped an arm around his neck. "I would like that," she murmured.

"It was just the two of you, with no other family, right?" he asked, giving her a wary look.

"No other family," she confirmed. "We were raised by our aunt and uncle, but they've been gone quite a few years now. So, it was just me. And, in the interest of transparency, don't forget that there's a good chance I can't have kids."

"I remember." He kissed her gently and asked, "So, we'll put that in the past as well, right?"

"We'll face the future though, right?" She narrowed her gaze at him, when he didn't respond right away.

He grinned. "Absolutely, but I really prefer to live in the present."

"Good, so do I. So, what is it we're living for?"

"How about for you and for me and for whatever it is that we've come together for," he suggested. "And, yes, I remember about the potential of not having kids, but I suspect that the minute we spend any time at Terkel's lovely castle, you'll find any concerns about fertility issues to be a thing of the past."

"I don't even know that I have fertility issues, but, if there was ever a place to overcome them," she noted, with a laugh, "Terk's headquarters would be it. And it's funny to even contemplate that it would be an answer and a solution. And you're okay with the possibility of no kids of our own?" She needed to hear him say it.

He nodded. "I'm okay with that," he replied in a soft tone. "We can always look at adoption or surrogates, if need be. Also remember how we will be surrounded by kids there. You know that, right? It might be hard on you."

She shook her head. "Remember what I do for a living?" she asked, laughing. "And I'm *sooo* looking forward to using all this newfound energy to help my patients."

He grinned and nodded. "Absolutely." He looked down at her for a moment, rubbing their noses back and forth, and added, "We could give it the old college try."

She looked up at him. "What are you talking about?"

"You know, that whole fertility thing? I mean, we haven't even gotten so far as to see if we're compatible yet."

"Oh, right, and we do need to see if that works for both of us," she agreed with a nod, trying to hold back her grin.

He smiled and then laughed openly. "I don't think we need any excuses now, do we?"

"No, we sure don't," she said, as she pulled him closer. "I think you should stop talking now."

He grinned, then lowered his head. Just this kiss was strong enough, deep enough, and passionate enough to make her toes curl. When he finally lifted his head, she was breathless and panting for more.

"Christ," she muttered. "You want to just repeat that over and over?"

"Yeah, I'll do my best," he whispered, his tone thick and heavy, then laid a second deep, heavy kiss on her. When he came up for air, he muttered, "Holy crap, we'll set these sheets on fire."

"That's okay. We're in a hotel. They have to replace them, not us."

He gave a muffled laugh and then kissed her deeply once again. By the time he was done, she was writhing beneath him, her body heated, softened, already opening for him. She groaned as she shifted her hands, trying to reach more of him, but he was holding her in such a way that she could hardly explore his body, even as he was working her nerves to shattered extinction.

When she finally got one hand free, she slid it through his dark hair, loving the feel of his silky curls, not curls but waves against her fingers, as he slowly trailed kisses down her cheek, her neck, then to her breast, before taking in the nipple and suckling it like a babe. She moaned as she arched up against him and whispered, "Jesus, I know it's been a while, but holy crap."

He smiled at her and asked, "Has it been a while?"

"Yes, damn it, apparently too long," she grumbled, as she shifted underneath him.

"Easy," he said, "we have all the time we want."

"That's nice for you, but I don't think I'll make it that long."

"Nobody said you had to," he teased, sliding his fingers between them and finding the soft moistness at her apex. When he gently slid one finger inside her, stroking in and out, she shattered, coming apart in his arms.

He smiled. "See? You didn't have to wait." And, with that, he did it again and again. When she cried out a second time, he rose over her, gently entering and waiting for her to look at him.

She looked up, dazed, and whispered, "Please."

He immediately slid all the way to the center of her. She gasped at the sudden fullness, shifting slightly to better accommodate him, as she opened her thighs wider and wrapped her legs tightly around his hips. Then he started to move. He didn't drive more than a few times before she came apart in his arms again, and then he lost control, driving for his own satisfaction now, deeper, faster, and harder, until she cried out yet again. A guttural groan escaped Riff, as his own orgasm ripped through him. She held him as he slowly sagged beside her.

She lay her head against his chest, as she waited for the cataclysmic shock waves still moving through her own body to ease back.

He held her close and asked, "Is it always like that for you?"

She shook her head. "No."

"That's okay," he said. "I'm more than happy to keep this up."

She smiled at him. "I sure hope so. When I said, *It's been a while*, I mean, it's been a really long while. As in, since my fiancé."

"Yeah, me too."

She looked at him in surprise, as he shrugged. "I was too messed up to even want to go in that direction again."

She leaned over and kissed him. "But the direction we're going now is the right one," she said.

He nodded and pulled her against him. "Exactly, and it's where we probably should have been in the first place, but, for whatever reason, we got off track."

She knew what the reason was—her sister and her energy tricks. Something Angela would have to examine closely but later. Much later. Right now they were on the right track, and her sister, for all her craziness, was hopefully at peace.

Angela wrapped her arms around Riff and whispered, "I might need to sleep for a minute or two."

"You can sleep for a lot longer than that. We have plenty of time. I'll be right here when you wake up."

She lifted her head to see his face, and he smiled. "I promise."

"Good enough," she whispered, as she kissed him, then sagged back down against his warm body and closed her eyes.

Knowing that the future had never looked brighter, she finally cuddled deeply in his arms and slept.

This concludes Book 15 of Terk's Guardians: Riff.
Read about Steele Trap, Book 1 of The Beacon

The Beacon: Steele Trap (Book #1)

Terk, driven by good intentions, crafts a defense system—powered by the energy of his team and their families, ensuring its purity. Designed to repel the enemy or to at least alert them of an approach, the system is now active. Yet, as with all energy, it grows, transforms, and, as Terk is discovering, *evolves*—just not in the way anyone anticipated …

Cyan, after years of planning, finally makes her unannounced visit to Terk and his team. Not specifying her arrival date and time leaves her to face unexpected barriers. Locks and unfamiliar woods stand in her way, and she curses her lack of foresight. As she navigates the dense forest, she encounters Steele, the man who saved her life eight years ago. Shocked and intrigued, she struggles to maintain her distance, her heart racing with unresolved emotions.

Steele, disoriented and lost, wanders through the woods, trapped in a surreal dreamscape. His memory is a blur, and he senses an unseen threat closing in. Confusion and fear grip him as he battles an invisible enemy, unaware of Cyan's presence and the connection that binds them.

When Steele is ambushed, Cyan comes to his rescue. Now, both are targets, desperate to reach the safety of Terk's place—a goal that proves far more elusive than they imagined.

Please continue reading for a sneak peek…

TERK MOVED CAUTIOUSLY through the dark but electric dreamscape, a sense of urgency tugging at him, something vital yet elusive. It danced just beyond his grasp, his mind struggling to pull him back, even as his consciousness whispered, *Wait, wait. We haven't quite got it.*

Normally he slept soundly, but lately something in the air felt off, inexplicable.

Only those like him could even begin to understand, yet this particular feeling seemed more significant than any from before. It involved him, his family, and their safety. The warnings were enough to make him cling to the dream, trying to hold on to the end. Yet it slipped through his fingers. Suddenly someone shook him awake, and he turned to see his beautiful wife, concern etched on her face. He frowned. She mirrored his expression.

He sighed, rubbing his eyes. "Whatever that dream was, it's important."

"Maybe," she replied softly, "but you're scaring the crap out of me."

He blinked, surprised.

"You were making wild noises and thrashing in bed." She gestured to the tangled bedcovers around his legs.

He groaned, untangling himself and then flattening against the pillows. "Sorry," he muttered, scrubbing his face as the wisps of the dreamscape already drifted away. "I wish I knew what the vision was all about."

Celia asked him, "Can you go back in with more detachment?"

"No, not likely," he muttered. "Not when it's important, not when it concerns our safety."

Her eyes widened, studying him. "Is something coming after us?"

He pondered her words. "That's not quite right, but something is definitely different."

Moments later, Wade, Ryland, Calum, and even Brody chimed in on their family channel, where they all could communicate together.

"Something weird is happening," Brody announced.

Ryland interjected, "I think a full alert needs to be sent out."

Terk swung his legs over the bed, sitting up swiftly. "Go back to sleep," he told his wife.

She raised an eyebrow, shaking her head. "Not if we're in danger."

"I don't know if we're in danger. I just know something's off."

"Good enough for me," she said, reaching for her robe and following him to the door. He frowned, but she nodded. "I'm going to the babies."

His expression softened. "And stay there, please."

Her eyebrows shot up. "If you're this worried, maybe we should warn everyone."

"All I can say is, something's wrong," he repeated, gently wrapping her up in a warm, caring hug. "It's not time for that level of panic yet."

Their voice channel suddenly buzzed with chatter, all filled with urgency.

"Meeting in the dining room now," Terk announced, silencing the clamor.

They had a shared wavelength for group communication via projected telepathy—a broadcasting of their thoughts to reach them all when needed in times of uncertainty—which was now overwhelming Terk as he headed to the dining room. He brewed coffee, knowing it would take multiple pots to satisfy everyone who would soon gather here. Visitors were common these days.

Returning with a full pot, Terk found his team awaited him. "I don't know what to tell you, but something's ..." He shrugged. "Something's off."

"Yeah, it's not just off," Ryland said quietly. "It's bizarre."

Surprised, Terk considered the energy source. "That's one word for it. Also... we might have an unexpected visitor."

"Not a friendly one, if this is the reception we're getting," Wade added.

"I'm not so sure," Ryland countered, glancing at Wade. "Something is here, but ... It sounds insane, but part of the threat – interference – energy – doesn't feel human."

The others stared.

Calum sank into a chair, holding out his empty cup. "Not human?" he repeated.

"I don't know yet," Terk replied. "I'm getting strange vibrations."

"Me too," Brody confirmed.

Terk noted all the men gathered here. The women were with the babies, prioritizing the children's safety.

When he mentioned it, the men nodded. "That's what we want, right?"

"It is."

"And if an attack is coming?"

"Where, why, how, and what's the purpose?" Terk asked.

The others were uneasy.

Calum added, "I don't like what you're suggesting."

"Maybe not, but ..." Terk shrugged and explained his dream. "I was close to finding out, but then I woke up."

"It's the Beacon," Ryland repeated, turning to Terk. "I'm sure of it. Something's going on with it."

The others closed their eyes, Terk included, all checking the Beacon. He blocked out any distractions and connected easily. Then he had built it, so he should have easy access. "The Beacon is there. It's functioning. Although ..."

"Yes, it is, but not well," Ryland insisted. "Something's wrong."

Terk wasn't sure *wrong* was the correct word here. He sensed something he'd never felt before. Never considered it a possibility. Still, his initial diagnostics showed everything was clear.

Calum added, "Ryland's right."

"It's working but not as intended," Terk stated, turning to his friend.

Calum shrugged. "It sounds crazy, but I think it's been tampered with."

"Nobody should be able to touch it," Terk noted. "We've added fail-safes. And we've put all our energies into it, making it, ... we thought, ... foolproof."

"Yet with more outside interest as our company grows," Calum suggested, "something's happening. I sense foreign energy."

The others nodded.

Brody agreed, "Yes, foreign energy."

"Not sure if it's good or bad. Is someone hurt?" Terk asked. "Is someone calling for help? Because that's a different issue altogether."

"The Beacon hasn't functioned at this level before. Maybe someone can't navigate it."

A soft knowing laughter echoed throughout the room.

Everyone stiffened, looking around.

"Did you hear that?" Calum asked in shock.

Terk nodded slowly. "I did." His mind raced. Was this an attack or something else? "I'll check the grounds. We built up the security around the castle because we needed to, but the woods? … That's a much harder area to keep track of."

"I'm coming with you," Calum offered.

Terk nodded. "Sounds good. Someone needs to stay here and be on watch."

"Absolutely," Ryland said. "I'll stay."

"And I'll join Calum and Terk," Wade volunteered.

Terk turned to the two men. "Be ready in five."

He quickly grabbed his shoes and a coat, reassured his wife, and stepped outside. As he moved, a sense of urgency pressed on him, like a closing window of opportunity. But, for what, he wasn't sure. It felt like his dream all over again, with that elusive knowledge slipping away.

Calum joined him, just as that same soft laughter rippled through the blackness of the night. "Did you hear that?" he whispered to Terk.

"I did, but I feel something else."

Calum added, "Not sure I like this."

The laughter rippled again.

"No. It's likely the Beacon." Terk frowned. "I know we

keep saying this."

Calum nodded. "Oh, I agree something is wrong with the Beacon. Not sure that's the correct word for what I'm feeling though." Then Calum turned to face the men, horror in his gaze.

"Honestly, it's wrong," Ryland said at his side, "but not how we're thinking about *wrong*."

Without breaking stride, Terk asked, "Meaning?"

Ryland winced. "I think the Beacon's been hijacked."

Terk stopped, as the truth slammed into his chest. "Dear God, … is it possible?" he whispered.

The other men turned, waiting.

"Not hijacked. I think …" Taking a deep breath, Terk finally said out loud the truth that had been ringing inside his head, one he was struggling to wrap his mind around. "I think the Beacon is evolving …"

Find Book 1 here!

To find out more visit Dale Mayer's website.

https://geni.us/DMSSteele

Author's Note

Thank you for reading Riff: Terk's Guardians, Book 15! If you enjoyed the book, please take a moment and leave a short review.

Dear reader,

I love to hear from readers, and you can contact me at my website: www.dalemayer.com or at my Facebook author page. To be informed of new releases and special offers, sign up for my newsletter or follow me on BookBub. And if you are interested in joining Dale Mayer's Reader Group, here is the Facebook sign up page.
http://geni.us/DaleMayerFBGroup

Cheers,
Dale Mayer

About the Author

Dale Mayer is a *USA Today* best-selling author, best known for her SEALs military romances, her Psychic Visions series, and her Lovely Lethal Garden cozy series. Her contemporary romances are raw and full of passion and emotion (Broken But … Mending, Hathaway House series). Her thrillers will keep you guessing (Kate Morgan, By Death series), and her romantic comedies will keep you giggling (*It's a Dog's Life*, a stand-alone novella; and the Broken Protocols series, starring Charming Marvin, the cat).

Dale honors the stories that come to her—and some of them are crazy, break all the rules and cross multiple genres!

To go with her fiction, she also writes nonfiction in many different fields, with books available on résumé writing, companion gardening, and the US mortgage system. All her books are available in print and ebook format.

Connect with Dale Mayer Online

Dale's Website – www.dalemayer.com

Twitter – @DaleMayer

Facebook Page – geni.us/DaleMayerFBFanPage

Facebook Group – geni.us/DaleMayerFBGroup

BookBub – geni.us/DaleMayerBookbub

Instagram – geni.us/DaleMayerInstagram

Goodreads – geni.us/DaleMayerGoodreads

Newsletter – geni.us/DaleNews